Mystery of the Museum
A Pip and Beth Detective Adventure

by
Ann Wilks

AuthorHouse™
1663 Liberty Drive
Bloomington, IN 47403
www.authorhouse.com
Phone: 1-800-839-8640

© *2011 by Ann Wilks. All rights reserved.*

No part of this book may be reproduced, stored in a retrieval system, or transmitted by any means without the written permission of the author.

First published by AuthorHouse   07/09/2011

ISBN: 978-1-4567-8235-1 (sc)

Printed in the United States of America

Any people depicted in stock imagery provided by Thinkstock are models, and such images are being used for illustrative purposes only.
Certain stock imagery © *Thinkstock.*

This book is printed on acid-free paper.

Because of the dynamic nature of the Internet, any web addresses or links contained in this book may have changed since publication and may no longer be valid. The views expressed in this work are solely those of the author and do not necessarily reflect the views of the publisher, and the publisher hereby disclaims any responsibility for them.

Dedicated to my grandchildren
Especially for Sophia

With love and thanks to
Derrick
For all your love, support, ideas and
encouragement

Contents

Prelude vii
Chapter 1   American Adventure 1
Chapter 2   The Castle 9
Chapter 3   Mystery Woman 18
Chapter 4   A Favourite Story 27
Chapter 5   Indians in the Forest 34
Chapter 6   Under the Stars 41
Chapter 7   The Search 50
Chapter 8   Hide! 58
Chapter 9   Whispers 64
Chapter 10   The Fort 70
Chapter 11   A Secret Place 77
Chapter 12   To the Rescue! 82
Chapter 13   Another Find 85
Chapter 14   The Runaway 93
Chapter 15   The Thief 99
Chapter 16   Truth Revealed 109
Finale 115
The Bedtime Stories 118

Prelude

Silently they approached the house, neither of them making a single sound as they crept through the undergrowth. They had left the heart of the forest yet as they neared the settlement, there were still enough trees to give cover. It was midsummer, and the branches were in full leaf. Moss and lichen grew underfoot, the peaty soil springing back into place as they passed, leaving hardly a footprint.

The day was almost over, evening was drawing in, and the heavy, deep shadows gave plenty of camouflage to the approaching figures. Both were in grey, the man from top to toe in grey hand-worked leather, the same colour as his companion.

As they stealthily drew nearer to the house their pace slowed. With a small movement of his hand the man gave a simple signal, and the animal crouched down. The man peered through the trees, furtively moving aside the deep green leaves on a lower branch, so that his view was not obstructed. At a second signal the animal dropped flat to the ground, his head resting on his huge paws. His yellow wolf's eyes glinting in the evening dusk appeared to be only half open, but at the first sign of movement behind the window a deep, guttural growl began in the depth of his throat. A warning glance from the Indian at his side was enough to silence him.

The long vigil had begun.

1

American Adventure

"The great beast made the last few steps into the deep shadows," the storyteller began. "He was swaying gently from side to side. It was dark beneath the tall, gently stirring branches of the trees. He came to a halt, without a word of command from his rider; he sensed that it was time to rest.

"Taking a firm hold of the bridle, and now giving the order to kneel, the traveller began to dismount. The night sky above him was twinkling with stars, but the sands, as he dropped down, still retained much of their ferocious daytime heat. 'A good time to set up camp,' he said to his nearest companion. 'We've come a long way today, yet there is still far to travel, before we reach our journey's end.' He turned to look away into the western sky, at one particular star that was shining brighter than anything else in the heavens."[1]

The warm summer breeze rustled the leaves in the potted palm beside Pip. He closed his eyes. He was enjoying the story and the soothing rocking motion of the swing. He could almost feel that he, too, was riding one of the swaying camels. He soon recognised the story, as the one about the Wise Men who came seeking Jesus, and as he listened he couldn't help thinking about the long journey that he had just done, that day. Here he was, sitting on the front porch of a house in America. It hardly seemed possible that this morning Nanna and Gramps had picked them up from their home in Liverpool to bring them here on a trip of a lifetime.

So here they were! It seemed amazing that at home it would be almost five o'clock in the morning, but here in America it was nine o'clock at night, and they were enjoying a bedtime story, told by a real cowboy.

It was getting quite dark when they had arrived at the house from the airport. The lights were on and the front door was wide open by the time the car came to a standstill. In the doorway was someone who looked exactly like a cowboy from TV. He was even wearing a big cowboy hat, and from that down to his silver-spurred boots he was dressed all in black; hat, shirt, belt, waistcoat, trousers, all were black, with lots of silver trimmings.

It was not until he took off his hat, and bowed low in welcome, that the children realised that his hair was also silver, and he was much older than Gramps. His face was all wrinkled and lined, and split by a huge friendly grin, as he walked down the steps to greet them.

Timothy, a man in his forties, who collected them from the airport, was the first to speak. "Dad," he began, "Let me introduce you. This is Pip and Beth, from England," he said, slipping an arm around both of their shoulders, and leading them up the wooden stairs. "And these are their grandparents," he added, smiling over to Nanna and Gramps. "Pip and Beth," he continued, "May I introduce my father, Zacchaeus Davidson, owner and curator of the Rose Davidson Memorial Museum."

The old cowboy laughed. "Oh, that sounds a bit too formal," he grinned. "All my friends call me Zac, so how about 'you-all' do that, too?" He spoke with a really broad American accent. "We're sure hoping 'you-all' are going to be our new friends from the Old Country. So come along in, and welcome to our home!" he continued, taking both children by the hand, and leading the way.

Although it had already been a very long day, Pip and Beth suddenly didn't feel tired any more, as they were shown to their twin bedded room, which had its own bathroom, 'en suite'. Timothy's wife, Bella May, had a lovely meal ready for them, but as they were eating Nanna began to notice that the children were getting rather weary.

"I'm afraid it will soon be bedtime," she said.

"Oh, Nanna," said Beth, "Can't we have a bedtime story?" she pleaded. Bedtime stories were always a feature of their holidays with their grandparents. Zac immediately looked interested, and suggested story time on the porch.

Most houses in America have seats on their front porches, and this was where Zac suggested they went. The porch was made of wooden decking, and ran the whole width of the house. It contained a couple of wicker chairs, a soft, old sofa, two or three wooden stools and an ancient swing, that would easily hold three or four people.

Pip and Beth made a beeline for the swing, and Zac sat between them. Timothy and his wife took the wicker chairs, and Nanna and Gramps sprawled out comfortably on the old sofa.

Zac looked round happily at his family and guests. "So today has been a day of travelling thousands of miles," he began, "And I think the tale of another long journey will be my choice for a bedtime story, tonight." He tipped his head far back and looked for a moment up into the evening sky. The sun was well on its way down, and there was just the glimmer of one or two stars coming out, twinkling in the deep blue above their seats. As he pushed slightly backwards, the swing picked up a gentle swaying motion, and Pip and Beth smiled in happy anticipation.

Pip really enjoyed the way Zac made the characters in the story come alive. There was even a camel, called George, who was very cantankerous, and didn't want to kneel down so that his owner could reload the treasure, the following morning; they had had to bribe him with a piece of date-bread.

As Zac drew his tale to an end, Nanna said, "Oh, that was a good story. My favourite bit is when they eventually find Jesus. The Bible says that they bowed down and worshipped Him."

"Yes, indeed," said Zac and he simply closed his eyes, as he continued, "Thousands of years ago, Lord, wise travellers sought Your Son, Jesus. Today our friends have travelled thousands of miles to visit and celebrate with us. Thank you for their safe arrival, and help us all to be those who still come and worship Him."

"Amen," said Gramps, with enthusiasm.

Pip woke to brilliant sunshine streaming in through the large glass doors near his bed. For a moment or two he felt disorientated, but when he turned the other way, and saw Beth, still fast asleep in her bed at the other end of the long room, he remembered.

It was just a year since he and Beth had solved the Mystery at the Manor, near Burnham on Crouch, and they had thought that that was the end of the matter, but it now seemed that it had only been the beginning. When they had got back home to Liverpool, there had been an e-mail from Professor Jackson at Burnham Museum, saying that he had just put their discovery onto the internet, and had already had a number of people contacting his site, asking for details. Most of them were from academics interested in the treasure they had found, but some, quite a few in fact, were from people asking for contact with the two "Treasure Hunters".

The professor had wanted to know if Pip and Beth were happy to have their contact details included on his site. After talking with their parents, and of course Nanna and Gramps, they had both agreed, never imagining that it would generate so much interest. Now, hardly a day went by without someone getting in touch. The most common contacts were from children who just wanted a few more details about how they had followed the clues to find the treasure, or wanted to say how much they had enjoyed reading about their discovery, but occasionally there was an e-mail from someone who wanted help with some mystery that they were trying to solve.

Then one day they had had an e-mail from the Rose Davidson Memorial Museum in the town of Astoria, Oregon, USA. Astoria was twinned with Burnham and their museum was celebrating its centenary, its hundred year anniversary, in July later that year. The founder of the museum had always encouraged young people to take an interest in local history, so when the present owner read on the website about them, he wanted to invite Pip and Beth to be his honoured guests for a couple of weeks and open the proceedings. It was to be an all-expenses-paid trip, for two adults and the two children. What he didn't say was that he had a mystery of his own that needed solving.

Their school felt that it would be a great educational opportunity for the children, and Nanna and Gramps were more than happy to take them, as their parents were too busy.

Pip had woken early and found that he was starving. He looked at his watch and could hardly believe it was only quarter to five. Why was he so famished? It would be ages before anyone was up for breakfast. Then he remembered that English time was eight hours later than his watch. No wonder he felt hungry, at home Mum and Dad would just be sitting down to lunch!

He tried to settle down, but what with the bright sunlight and his rumbling tummy, not to mention the birds outside, which had decided to wake up too, there was no chance of going back to sleep. He remembered that Mum had packed some crisps in his carry-on bag, in case 'there wasn't enough to munch on the plane', but there had been lots to eat yesterday. He looked across at Beth, and decided that crunching crisps would probably disturb her.

He pulled on his dressing gown, picked up his bag and went over to the glass doors. They opened onto a veranda, overlooking the back garden. A couple of wooden chairs and a table were on the balcony, so he quietly closed the door and sat down. The crisps had somehow slipped right down the side of the bag, so he thought it would be best to tip everything out to find them. He soon spotted the bright green cheese and onion ones he liked.

While he was eating he looked about him. There were a number of houses down the street, each of them had large gardens. As he looked out here at the back, though, there were no fences; all the gardens ran together, towards a little stream, which seemed to be a boundary, as other houses with their plots led up from the water to the next road. All around the stream were a number of trees, large and small and even on this warm sunny morning there were deep shadows under them.

He was just finishing the last few crumbs when his gaze rested on the things he'd tipped onto the table. Among the usual things like his mobile and an old Gameboy there was a dark green box. He smiled to himself as he opened it, remembering how surprised his parents had been that he and Beth had decided to spend the first of their reward money buying a Bible. Carefully now he lifted the new book, with its golden edged pages out of the box and placed it on the table. He had planned to read something from it everyday while he was on holiday, and this seemed as good a time as any. Nanna had suggested that the New Testament was a good place to start, as it told the stories about

Jesus. He remembered how much he had enjoyed Zac's story the night before, so he decided he would try to find it.

Pip flicked through the book until he found the index. The books in the list were divided into two, the Old and New Testaments. The second list began with Matthew, and told him which page to find. It didn't take him long. Matthew started with a great long list of names, called 'The Genealogy of Jesus', he didn't think there could be anything interesting there, so he skipped on to the next heading, about the birth of Jesus.

'Nearly there,' he thought, turning over to see that Chapter Two began with 'The Visit of the Magi'. He knew that that was one of the names Zac had used to describe the Wise Men, so he settled down in the warm sun to read. He found it interesting that the Wise Men had been warned by a dream not to return to Herod with news of where they had found the baby.

'I wish I had dreams like that,' he thought. The title of the next section 'Escape to Egypt' sounded exciting, and had another warning of danger in it. He was soon so engrossed in the story that Beth had to call him twice to tell him to get ready for breakfast.

And what a breakfast it was! They were soon all sitting around the large kitchen table, enjoying mounds of pancakes. There were all sorts of things to add to the pancakes; maple syrup was the most popular, but there were also jams, which the Americans called jelly, peanut butter, ham, bacon and scrambled eggs. Beth thought that it seemed really strange that the Americans put all of these things on their plates at the same time, whereas the English way was to begin with the savoury things first, and then move onto the sweet things. Nanna said they shouldn't think of American ways as wrong, just different. She thought it might be fun to try some things the American way, but even so, she shook her head when Pip began to drizzle maple syrup over his bacon covered pancake.

"Mmm, lovely," he said, laughing at the reaction on her face. "You should try it!"

She just shuddered, and decided to ask the question that had been bothering her since they entered the kitchen.

"I can still hardly believe we're here," she said. "But I've been wondering, what exactly are we supposed to do, you know, at the celebrations?" she asked.

"It's difficult to imagine that we should be anyone's Honoured Guests," Pip said, voicing just what Beth had been thinking.

"Well," began Zac, "On Independence Day, the 4th of July, there will be a parade through the main street of town, and we are hoping that you will lead the march. Then there will be a huge party, in the afternoon. There will be all sorts of competitions. You might like to take part in some of them, and we'd like you to give out the prizes."

"Wow!" the children said together.

"And in the evening there will be an enormous firework display in the museum grounds," added Zac.

"It sounds great," said Beth.

Pip nodded. "So, does the museum belong to you?" he asked. "Last night Timothy said you were the owner and curator, didn't he?"

"That's right. It has been in the family since it was built," answered Zac. It was started by Isaac, who was my great-grandfather, in honour of his mother, Rose. She was probably the most famous of all the Davidsons. Everybody here in Astoria has heard of her."

Timothy took up the story. "She began to work in the lumber trade, seemingly as soon as she arrived here, from the UK. She was the best employer in the district and by the end of her short life she was paying the highest wages in the area, providing better healthcare and a better education for her workers' children. She was well known for her kindness even to the local Indians, at a time when others were persecuting them."

"Her son, Old Isaac," continued Zac, "Obviously adored her. She died of TB when he was just in his teens. These days tuberculosis is one of the illnesses that most children are given their jabs for, but in those days many people died from it. When Isaac took over the building of the big house, which is now our museum, he filled the place with memories of his mother."

"It's a good thing that he did, because apart from them we simply can't find out much about Rose at all," went on Timothy. "Where was she from, how did she get here? There are so many questions but there just aren't many records."

"No, not many at all," went on Zac. "The front page of the family Bible begins with just two names, John and Rose on the top line. And Rose herself remains a woman of mystery. In fact," he continued, "I have to confess that part of my reason for inviting you over here was that I hoped you might be able to unravel some of the mystery surrounding her."

"Oooo!" said the children in unison, exchanging smiles.

"We'd love to help!" Said Pip.

"We have all heard so much about the other mystery you solved," put in Bella May.

"They certainly seem to have a knack for it," said Gramps, proudly. He had not been too enthusiastic initially, but in the end he'd seen that both Pip and Beth had proved to be good at following clues, and coming up with the right answers.

Zac looked around the table at all the empty plates, "So, what are we waiting for?" he asked. "Let's get started. Come and see!"

2

The Castle

Zac drove the short distance to the museum, and Pip and Beth found it really strange travelling on the 'wrong' side of the road. Soon they drew up outside a large building set back a long way from the road with a huge grassy area at the front and the forest coming almost down to one side of the house.

The locals always referred to the Rose Davidson Museum as 'The Castle', but it wasn't a castle at all, at least nothing that the children would have called a castle in England. For a start it really didn't look that old. It was a square building, with four storeys; it was very symmetrical, with four windows on each floor. At both of the front corners there were rounded rooms, topped by conical roofs. It was probably this feature that made it appear to be a small castle.

As they walked up the driveway, Pip and Beth read the large sign by the open front door. It said, 'Welcome to the Rose Davidson Memorial Museum. Step inside to experience life in nineteenth century Astoria. Open Monday to Saturday, 10-4pm.'

On the other side of the door was a large blue and red sign, brand new, and reading, 'Join us for our Centenary Rendezvous, here, July 1st-7th, Native American Drums and Dancers, Craft Stalls, and Competitions. Come and meet our special English Treasure Hunters.'

Once again the children exchanged smiles, they could hardly wait. Zac had told them that there would be plenty of new things for them to try, like how to use tomahawks, throwing knives and even black powder guns. Pip was keen to improve his skill with bow and arrows.

"What's a Ren . . . Ren?" asked Beth, struggling with the long word on the board.

"Rendezvous?" guessed Zac. He made it sound like 'Ron-day-voo'. "Well, that is a very special part of our celebrations," he explained. "Here on the lawns of the museum lots of people are going to be living like we did in the 1840's. There will be tents and Indian tipis." He made that word sound like 'teepees'; it is the name for the special round white Native Americans' tents. "We will be going into the forest one day soon, to borrow a real Indian tipi from a friend of ours, for you to sleep in next week."

Pip and Beth exchanged glances, they always loved camping, but this was going to be even more special. They were really looking forward to this part of their holiday.

Zac took them inside the building. On their left hand side there was a booth, where ordinary visitors would have to pay, but of course they wouldn't. Zac went straight up to the glass window.

"Hello there, Peter," he said, "I've brought you some fellow travellers from across the Atlantic. They are to visit here anytime they like, as our guests, of course!" The man smiled.

Zac turned to Pip and Beth, "Here is Peter Barrowclough, my deputy curator, who is also from England. He's been ever so helpful since he arrived a few months ago."

They all said hello, and Gramps immediately recognised his well-loved Yorkshire accent.

"Well, well," he said, "I didn't expect to find a Yorkshireman right over here in the West of America. What brings you to Astoria?"

"I've been on the trail of the early explorers," explained Peter. "This part of America was one of the last to be discovered. I flew into New York and heard the story of two adventurers, called Lewis and Clarke, who were the first white men to come here. They journeyed all across America, with their Indian guide, and built a fort near Astoria. I'd been following in their footsteps, and I liked Astoria so much, I thought I'd stop awhile."

"And very pleased we are to have you," said Zac, with enthusiasm. "We'd been having a few problems here at the museum, and I felt I needed someone to give me a hand. We even had a burglary, just before Peter arrived, which is almost unheard of in these parts. So when Peter came along, with his love of history and an offer to help, I was only too pleased.

"But come along, now, let me show you around."

They left Peter and Gramps chatting happily together and the rest of them entered the huge hallway, from which other doors opened into the various rooms on that floor. An enormous staircase, which came down the centre, dominated the hall and then at a half-landing it split in two, both arms of the stairs sweeping down either side of the entrance.

"Wow!" said Beth, looking up. "That's gigantic!"

Zac smiled, and led them on.

They walked straight through, under the stairwell, until they stood in front of a vast ornate fireplace, which had a bright wood fire burning, even on such a sunny day. Fire irons made from brass were hanging, sparkling beside the roaring fire, and there was a very long poker and a toasting fork. Zac took down the poker and gently moved the logs to give off a little more heat.

Beth was looking at the clock, which took pride of place in the centre of the mantelpiece. It was massive, standing more than a metre high. It was in the form of two brass figures, a mother walking in the countryside with her young son. The sculptor had captured forever a very special moment in time. Beth thought that their flowing robes and their looks of delight as they explored together were very realistic. The mother was pointing to a fluffy bee, which had landed to collect the nectar from a delicate flower. Beth could tell that it was a wild rose, even though the brass was all a dark brown colour. As the mother was bending towards her son their heads almost met, and the boy's chubby fingers reached out towards her long, curling hair. In her other hand the mother was carrying a banjo, and the rounded body of the musical instrument had been very cleverly turned into the face of the clock.

Beth noticed that the hours were marked with the Roman numerals, and she smiled to herself; last year Pip had shown her how to read them, so this year she could understand them, too. The two brass figures were standing on a little mound; the leaves of grass were bending lightly, as if under the pressure of a gentle breeze. At the base of the clock there were two beautifully written words, which were not in English. Beth struggled to read the words; she thought they might be Latin. Nanna had told them about Latin flower names last year, and she thought these words were similar to some of those.

"What does it say?" she asked Nanna, pointing.

"Tempus fugit," she answered. "Time flies."

"Well, now," said Zac, "Time will be flying away with us, if we don't get a move on. I think we've warmed up nicely, so shall we go?"

They all nodded.

"We'll start in the library," he suggested. "It's the first room on the left-hand side of the entrance," he said to Pip, letting the children lead the way.

The library was in one of the round, turret rooms at the corner of the building, which meant that it had three large windows, letting in lots of golden sunlight. They turned into the doorway, and then both children hesitated. It seemed that the room was occupied; a woman and child were seated at a table by the front window, poring over a book together. They didn't seem to have heard the children entering, and didn't move as Zac ushered them in. He smiled at Nanna, and then paused for a moment, to watch the children's reaction. Pip was the first to realise that the figures were not people at all, but dummies, dressed in old-fashioned clothes.

"Oh, Zac," he said, "You might've told us. We thought we were disturbing someone at their reading!"

By now Beth had grasped the situation, and she smiled. She looked over at Zac, whose tough old face was creased with laughter lines. "You did that on purpose!" she said, laughing. "That's why you let us come in first!"

Zac laughed outright. "Couldn't resist it!" he said, his eyes sparkling. "All through the house," Zac told them, "Old Isaac set out the rooms to illustrate some of the things he remembered most about his mother. She taught him to read, and he said that they spent many happy hours together with books. When he first made the museum, Old Isaac used life sized cardboard cut-outs. These days we have replaced them with manikins.

"Each room has the figures of Rose and Isaac doing something together, something that he remembered them enjoying during his childhood. He looked back with such fondness on his memories, but he realised that not everyone was as fortunate as he had been. Many parents don't spend much time with their children." At this Pip looked over at Beth; they knew what he meant. "So here in the museum he wanted to suggest to his visitors ways that parents and children could spend time together. The different rooms kind of tell the story of him growing up here in Astoria. We will have a look at them, later."

The walls of the library were filled with books of every shape and size. There were freestanding bookcases too, and in the middle of the room there was a glass display case, which held an open Bible. Zac walked over to it.

"Our family tree is in here," said Zac, opening the lock on the glass case with one of the many keys that he carried on his huge key ring. He lifted the large, black, leather-bound book carefully onto an empty table, so that the children could get a better look at it. They moved round to see better, and Zac and Nanna looked over their heads.

The Bible had been opened towards the middle, but Zac turned it back to the first page, which was headed "Our Family". Dotted lines had been printed across the page, for people to fill in with their family details. As Zac had told them at breakfast time, the first two names at the top of the page, had been carefully written in, John and Rose. There were no dates beneath them to indicate when they were born, when they had got married or even the dates when they died. This was quite different from the other names on the page. When the children looked at those they saw that all of them had details underneath them, sometimes recording the place where they were married, as well as a date.

"I see what you mean about there not being much information about Rose," said Pip. "And she was your great-great-grandmother?" he asked.

"That's right," said Zac. Then he pointed to the next line on the page. "And here is Old Isaac, my great-grandfather. He was such a great character."

"Did you ever meet him?" asked Beth, noticing the way Zac's eyes crinkled at the corners, as he spoke of the old man.

"Meet him?" Zac said, in amazement. "Of course I met him! I used to spend all my vacations here with my grandparents."

Beth was surprised, "That's just like we do!" she said, looking over at Nanna.

Zac nodded. "By the time I was six-years-old Old Isaac had come to live with my grandparents and we had such a lot of fun together," Zac told them. "It was still such a wild country, in those days, what with real cowboys in the town, and lumberjacks and the Indians in the forest. You never knew what was going to happen next!

"Old Isaac realised that I liked to hear the stories of his childhood, and he told me all he could remember. But even he didn't know anything about Rose's past. So you see she is a real mystery woman. But then, you have experience of mysteries, haven't you?"

Nanna saw the excitement in their faces. "Solving this mystery might give you something else to do while you are here," she said.

She had hardly finished speaking when they all heard a mournful howl, coming from the trees just through the window. Despite the warmth of the day a cold chill went down Beth's spine.

"What, what was that?" asked Pip; his eyes wide open.

"That?" asked Zac, "That . . . was a wolf," he answered.

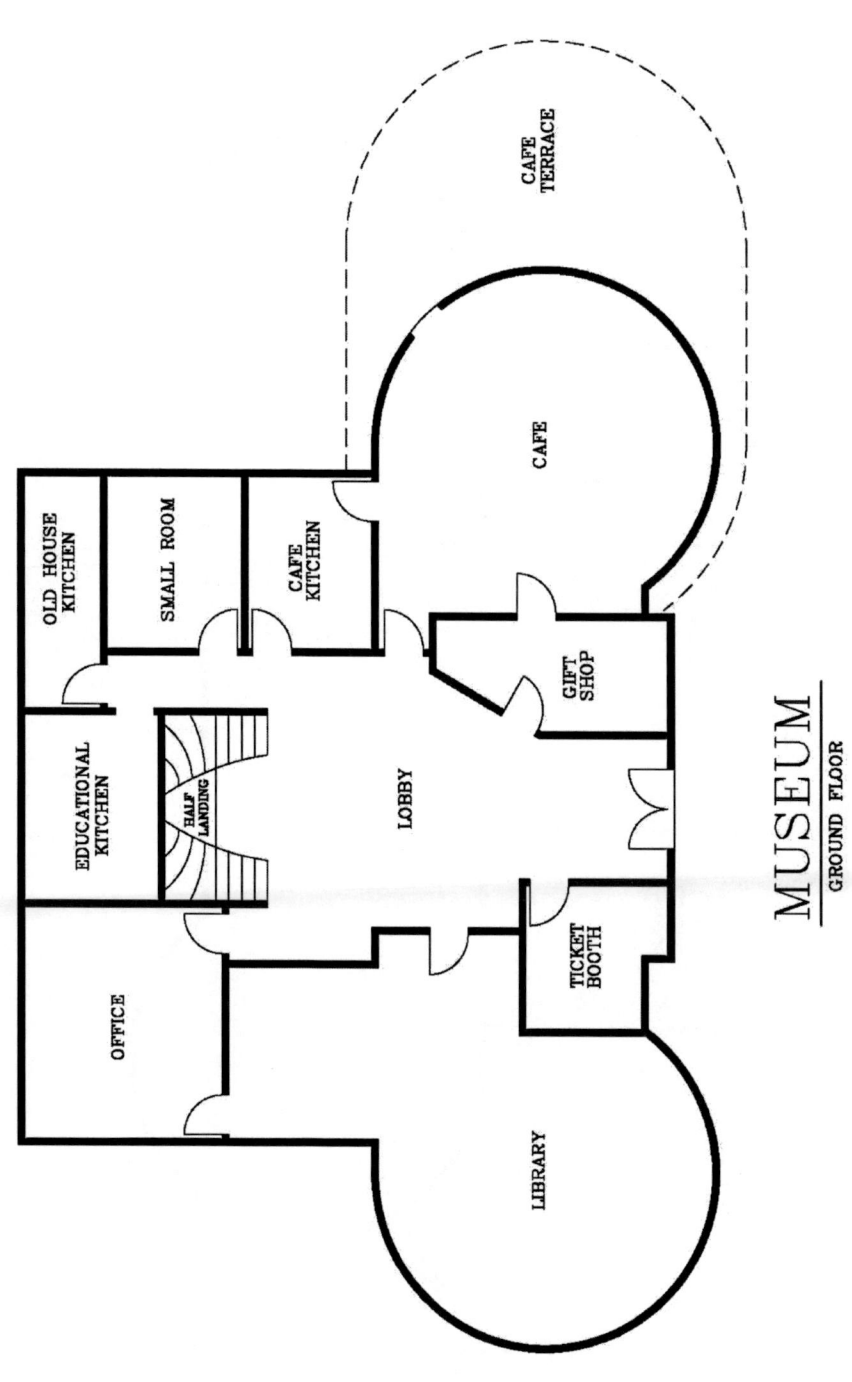

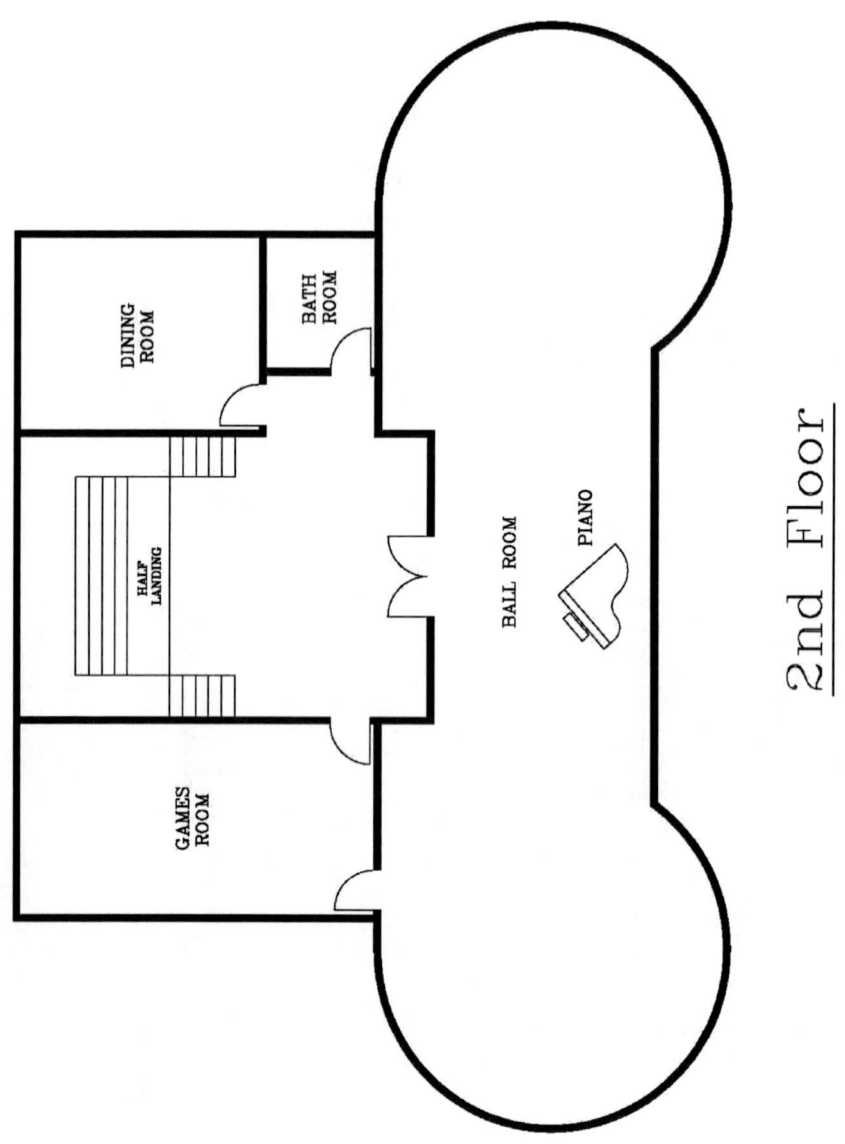

2nd Floor

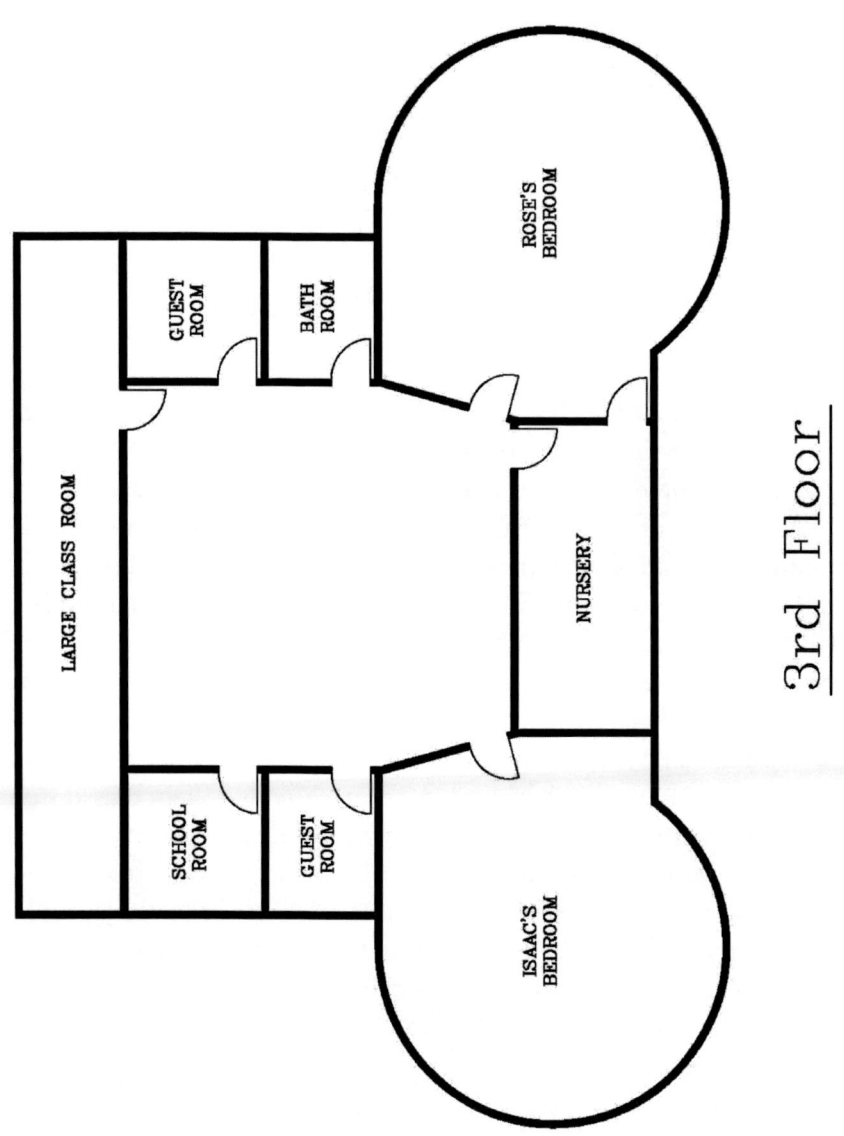

3

Mystery Woman

Zac suggested that they leave the library, and go on a tour of the rest of the house. This time he led the way, and Pip and Beth took delight in finding the different dummies that represented Rose and Isaac.

At the back of the house there was a small kitchen. Here the female dummy was wearing what looked like a maid's outfit, a dark blue dress, under a large white apron. She was baking at the table, with a little boy of about four years old, who had his hands in the bowl with her. There was flour all over the table—they had obviously been having a great deal of fun. The plaque by the entrance read 1866.

Through a door at the back of the kitchen was another room, also laid out as a kitchen, but a much bigger one. Zac told them that at first Old Isaac had intended the museum to be mainly a family experience, but as the museum got more and more popular schools from miles away began to visit, so he had created areas where school children could enjoy interacting with members of staff in activities, like cooking, gardening and lessons in the large upstairs schoolroom.

Next Zac took them to one of the small downstairs rooms, where Rose was shown dressed in travelling clothes, carrying a baby in her arms. She held a carpetbag in her other hand. Zac said it represented their arrival at Astoria in 1863. "But like we said at breakfast, we don't know exactly where she came from, though we do know she was English."

"But that does give us the date when Rose came here," said Beth. "Perhaps I should just make a note of that," she added, digging around in her bag to get her pad and pencil out. She wrote '1863 arrived in Astoria' under the heading 'Rose Davidson'.

Zac smiled as he led them on.

The office at the back of the museum looked out onto the abandoned sawmills, large timber buildings, almost in the tree line. At the office desk there were two chairs, again with dummies showing Rose apparently this time teaching Isaac what was involved in the running of the business. The plaque read 1874.

"So Isaac would have been twelve years old," said Pip.

"That's right," said Zac, "Just twelve years old and already learning the business side of things. Up till then Rose had taught him at home, but soon he was to go away to school in Portland. It was at about the age of twelve that Rose began to shorten Isaac's name to Zac. Most people called him that, but when I came along as a baby he became Old Isaac, and I became the only Zac in the family.

"But enough of that, let's go upstairs now, and continue our tour."

They mounted the stairs, and at the half-landing they took the right flight of steps, to the dining room. Here the dummies showed Rose and Isaac eating together.

"Five-year-old boys would normally still be eating in the nursery, but Rose wanted to have him with her as much as possible," said Zac. "It is almost as though she knew that their time together would be short."

On leaving the dining room Zac took them into the billiard room, and here a nine-year-old Isaac was playing with his mother.

"It might have been a man's sport in those days," commented Zac, "But Rose always seemed to excel in a man's world."

Next he took them into the ballroom, which took up the whole of the front of the second floor. It was the largest room in the museum. It had been decorated in all its Christmas splendour. Zac explained how Old Isaac had told him that it was one of his last memories of his mother. She was wearing a beautiful lemon coloured crinoline dress, very full in the skirt. The young fourteen-year old Isaac was looking very smart in black trousers and jacket with a white shirt; he was even wearing a black satin dickey bow. They were getting everything ready for their annual Christmas Ball for their employees.

"Isaac remembered nearly everything about those Christmas holidays," said Zac. "He told me that Rose was always tired. He teased her about it one day, and compared her unfavourably with his classmates at school. She seemed pleased that he was happy in Portland, and he noticed that she had a contented 'glow', as he described it. It wasn't until years later, long after Rose had died, that Isaac remembered this and realised that that was one of the later symptoms of TB. At the time he thought it was all part of the happiness she was feeling. She had only recently become a Christian. One of the missionaries who came to work with the Indians she loved had told her all about Jesus, in a way that she had never heard before. Isaac said she seemed to be at peace. She told him that the Christmas carols meant so much more to her, that year; she was always playing them on the piano over there, under the window."

They all looked over to the shiny, black grand piano, lit up in the morning sunlight.

"I love Christmas carols, too," said Nanna, as she walked over to take a closer look at the instrument.

Beth went up to take a proper look at the dress. It went almost down to the floor, longer than the other dresses in the house, which all showed the ankles and shoes and were practical for working in.

Pip hadn't time for that, and was eager to see the rest of the house, so they were all soon climbing the steps to the third floor, where there were the sleeping quarters and schoolroom. Zac explained that these were the last rooms on show. The fourth floor was just an attic storeroom, now, although it had been the servants' quarters years ago, and had its own set of stairs at the back of the house.

In the nursery there was a baby in a crib, with the mother sitting rocking the cot with her foot while reading from a great big, brightly coloured children's bedtime storybook. Next to that, in one of the big round rooms, was Isaac's bedroom. Here a ten-year-old and his mother played on the floor with a miniature railway.

In the schoolroom, the mother was at the blackboard, writing out something with white chalk.

"What is it, that Rose is writing?" asked Beth.

Zac looked over at the lettering on the board. "Ah, yes!" he exclaimed. "She and Old Isaac loved doing puzzles together, so he thought it would be fun to put one of his favourite ones up in here, so that the school children could have a go at solving it. Can you work it out?"

The children looked carefully and this is what they saw:

Y Y U R

Y Y U B

I C U R

Y Y 4 me.

"Well I never!" exclaimed Nanna, in amazement. "Would you believe it? That is one of the first puzzles my great-grandfather showed me, when I was a little girl."

"It must have been popular, at the time," said Zac. "I know Old Isaac always said he remembered it well, and of course he was my great-grandfather, too."

"Have you two worked it out?" Nanna asked the children.

"How do you mean, work it out?" asked Beth. "It just seems to be a load of letters."

"Wait a minute," said Pip, "I was just thinking that the third line looks a bit like some of the texts I send to my friends, on my mobile. I often send CU instead of 'see you', don't you, Beth?"

"Of course," said Beth, looking again at the letters. "But they didn't have mobiles in those days."

"No," said Zac, "But it was just a kind of code, for fun."

"So I get the endings of the lines," said Beth, "But why are there two 'Y's . . . Oh, I see!" she suddenly said, as the penny dropped.

As she had said "Two 'Y's" it sounded like 'too wise', which of course was what it meant.

Pip got it at the same moment, so they both ended up saying it together, much to Zac and Nanna's amusement.

"Too wise you are

Too wise you be

I see you are

Too wise for me!"

"How clever!" said Beth, "Even if it's a bit old fashioned, it's sort of like a poem."

"Well, it's a bit more interesting than just doing sums," said Pip, looking at the dummy of the eight-year-old Isaac, sitting at his desk, with slate and chalk in front of him, and a mathematical sum to solve.

"Old Isaac said they had lots of fun, working out clues like that," said Zac. "It's good to see that you two are good at solving puzzles, too."

He led the way out of this small room and then into a much larger schoolroom, fitted out with a dozen desks, complete with slates and chalks, for the modern school children to try out education nineteenth-century-style.

The last room that Zac took them into was Rose's own bedroom. Pip and Beth were surprised when they were talking about the visit later, to realise that they had both felt that it was the saddest part of the house. The room was dim; the curtains were drawn. The dummy was sitting in bed, leaning back on the pillows. Even though it was a dummy, the face was very pale.

They hardly needed Zac to explain that this was the room where Rose had died. There was a piece of half-finished embroidery in her lap, and on the table nearby was a tinted picture of Isaac in school uniform. He looked smart in his dark blue blazer and pale blue shirt; he looked very serious and it seemed fitting that in those days people did not smile when they had their photographs taken. Beside the photo was a small jewellery box and an open Bible.

"So Rose died in 1876," said Beth, reading the plaque, by the bed.

"That's right," said Zac.

"And her Zac was fourteen," put in Pip, proudly, before Beth could say anything.

"He was!" exclaimed their Zac, smiling.

Beth was looking at the embroidery laying across the dummy's hand. "What is that, on her knee?"

"Well," began Zac, "Among the most precious personal possessions that were Old Isaac's was a piece of embroidery. It has now been framed." He pointed over to the wall. "But Isaac wanted to show her sewing it. Apparently this was the very last thing that Rose made," Zac told the children. "During her final winter, as she was dying of consumption, TB as we know it today, the servants told him that every day she made herself complete just a few more stitches, until finally it was finished, just a few days before Isaac was due home from school. Unfortunately she died the very day it was completed, and never saw her beloved son again. Isn't it sad?" Zac asked.

"Sure is," said Pip. He and Beth gazed down at the dummy, feeling quite sad themselves. Then Pip walked over to the embroidery on the wall. "And it's a bit of a funny present to make for a boy," he went on. "I wouldn't want a bit of sewing."

"But it is so beautifully done," said Beth, joining him. "Look at all those tiny stitches. It must have taken ages."

"I suppose it must," said Zac wandering over. "I had never thought about that." Like Pip, he too had never shown much interest in sewing.

"So," mused Beth, "If it took her so long to do, and if, like you say, Pip, it's a strange present for a boy, there must have been some really important reason for her to do it, mustn't there?"

"Must there?" asked Pip.

"Something very important," insisted Beth looking him straight in the eye.

Pip looked blank.

"Oh! I see what you mean!" exclaimed Zac. "It must have been very important to her."

"And it might be something important for us," said Beth, "Something to do with the mystery of who she was."

They all moved closer to the embroidery, now. Zac had looked at the sampler, as it was called, many times before, but he realised that actually he had never really looked at it properly. Now he took it down from the wall, and moved over to the window, so that they could all look at it carefully.

At the top of the picture was a quaint old poem. There was lettering all around the edges, the alphabet down one side, and numbers and more letters on the other. In the middle of the picture was a house. It was an imposing three-storey building, made of grey stone. There was a large porch over the front door, which was flanked by four long windows on each side. The windows above these were smaller than those on the ground floor, but not as tiny as the nine windows of the attic floor above. There was a driveway leading straight to the front door; poplar trees lined each side of the drive and smooth green lawns surrounded it, broken only by a sundial on the left hand side and a stone birdbath on the right. This house was unlike anything they had yet seen in America.

Beautiful grey-green leaves and tiny pink flowers were twisting and trailing up from the two bottom corners to frame this picture of a house. Beth, who had this year been studying herbs and medicinal plants at Guides, recognised the plant straight away.

"That's rosemary, the herb," she said.

"Well done!" said Zac,.

"Oh, Beth is really good at recognising flowers and herbs," said Nanna, "And that one is quite unusual."

"Yes," said Zac "Old Isaac always thought that it was strange, because he said his mother hated rosemary, both the flowers and the herb. This is the only place in the house that has rosemary in it."

"Yet, we're thinking now that things in this picture are important," said Pip. "We need to remember this," he added, looking at Beth.

"I've been writing a few things, already," she said, digging her pad out of her shoulder bag again.

"So put that down," instructed Pip. "Rose hated rosemary, but put it on the sewing."

"You might want to copy the writing, too," said Zac, indicating the poem at the top, which read:

Where mother and son
Stoop to admire it
Banjo is playing
Tempus Fugit.

Pip had noticed that under the poem there was a picture of a key. Beneath the picture of the house were some words that they couldn't quite make out. Beth wrote down the letters she could recognise.

TH?I?TI??AM

Down the left-hand side of the sampler was simply the alphabet, going from A to Z, however the numbers and letters that ran down the right hand side were not so easy to recognise, and something inside Beth told her this could be another clue, and with slightly shaky hands she carefully copied them down, into her book.

10 9 8 7 6 5 4 3 2 1 S A A C L U K E 1 9 V 8 4 M E

When she had finished writing Zac replaced the sampler on the wall and they walked out onto the landing. They began to descend the stairs until they all seemed to come to a halt by the large back window that overlooked the gardens. Zac pointed outside and they could just see a fountain by the fishpond and a statue of two figures bending close together.

"That's six-year-old Isaac," he said. "There's a boy and his mother. She is showing him how to use a fishing rod."

"You said she was good at all sorts of sports," said Beth. "Gramps taught Pip how to fish, last year."

As they were looking down from the window, and Pip caught a movement in the corner of his eye, way over in the edge of the trees a dark shadow seemed to draw back under the branches. The same cold chill he had felt before when the wolf had howled ran down his spine.

"There's someone watching us, over there," he said.

Beth looked, and saw some of the lower branches moving, but she didn't see anyone. There wasn't any breeze around that day, yet the branches seemed to be swaying. "Over there?" she asked, pointing.

"I think so, but I'm not sure," continued Pip. "It looked like a grey figure, moving through the trees."

"I didn't see anyone," said Zac. "But sometimes people do think they are being watched, when they look out from here."

"Watched?" asked Beth. "Who would be watching?"

"Well, I don't know," said Zac. "This used to be an ancient Indian hunting ground, long before the Davidson Sawmills were built, and many people say that they can sometimes feel the Indians, watching them from the surrounding trees. It's a load of nonsense, though, because most of the Indians moved onto the Reservation years ago, and anyway, there wouldn't be a reason for them to be watching the museum, would there?" he asked.

"I suppose not," said Pip, "But you did say that there had been some strange happenings, the burglary and things." He was still positive that he had seen someone. There were certainly lots of deep, dark shadows beneath the trees, even on a sunny day.

As they turned away from the window, Pip was sure that he once more heard the baleful howling of a wolf. He shook his head, and followed the others down the stairs. He remembered his Bible reading that morning. There seemed to have been lots of warnings of danger. Could this be a kind of warning for him? Could they be in danger? 'Surely not!' he thought; this mystery was simply to find out information about Rose. There couldn't be any danger here, could there? Then he remembered, he had said that to himself last year and yet in the end that mystery had brought them into unexpected danger. What surprises did this holiday hold for them?

4

A Favourite Story

As they came down the stairs to the entrance again, they could hear Gramps and Peter still chatting away about places they had both been to in Yorkshire.

"You two are still at it, I hear," said Zac, smiling. "Well, if you have done enough talking, we were getting rather hungry, so we thought we would go into our coffee shop."

"I'm always ready for a coffee," said Gramps.

"Well, come along then," said Zac. "It's just through the gift shop in the other round-walled turret."

Gramps waved goodbye to Peter, "I'm sure we'll 'ave a chat agen another day," he said, following the others.

The little shop was full of all sorts of interesting things, from beads to bows and arrows, but the children were really feeling quite hungry, now, so they didn't stop to take a proper look. As Zac had said, they had plenty of time for that, later.

Pip and Beth had seen the Starbuck's coffee shop in central Liverpool at home, but the prices were very high, so they had never been inside. Pip's friends had told him about the amazing iced coffees, called Frapachinos, so he was looking forward to trying one.

"Well," said Zac, placing a cheese sandwich and a chocolate muffin on his tray, from the display counter, "It's such a sunny day, why don't we all go and eat at the tables outside?"

"Good idea," said Gramps. He ordered a ham sandwich and some chips. He was surprised when the waitress asked him which chips he wanted.

"Just a portion of chips," he said, puzzled.

"A portion of . . ." she began, "Oh, you mean you would like some fries with your sandwich?" she asked.

"Fries? Err, yes fries," said Gramps, suddenly realising what she meant. "I forgot that you call them that."

"So what are chips?" asked Beth, curious to know. Zac pointed to the display of crisps, next to the counter.

"Oh, here we go," said Pip, "We'll have to make our own English/American dictionary. Chips are fries, and crisps are chips, I wonder how many other new meanings we'll find!" They all laughed.

"You'll soon get the hang of it!" said Zac, telling the cashier to put the bill on the museum account. "These are our guests of honour for the celebrations. They are going to be presenting the prizes and telling us how they solved their mystery in England!"

"I can't wait!" she said enthusiastically.

"This is just fantastic," said Beth, carefully carrying her tray.

"So have you had a good morning?" asked Gramps, when everyone had got sorted out with lunch, and they were seated around a metal table, out in the sunshine.

Everyone was chatting about all the different things they had seen, and then when they had all finished, and the table was cleared, Beth took out her sketchpad, so they could all have a look at the wording on the sampler. Zac explained that there were a few things he needed to prepare for the celebrations, so he left them to themselves.

Gramps was amused that the children seemed to have found themselves another mystery for the holidays. Still, he remembered that last year they really had solved the clues and found some treasure, so he thought he had better take them a bit more seriously, this time. He asked to have a look at what Beth had written.

She passed the paper towards him, and as she did so her hand was covering the first few numbers. Suddenly something seemed to make sense. What she could now see was this,

1 S A A C L U K . . .

"Why," she said, immediately, "Those letters almost look like Isaac!"

When Beth moved her fingers Gramps could see that what he had thought at first glance to be a letter I, was really the number 1, at the end of all the other numbers.

Pip was sitting closest to Gramps, so he peered over to get a better look. "It does, rather," he said, "And the next bit looks like another name."

"You could be right, there," added Gramps. "It might be Luke."

"Well," said Pip, "We know that Rose's son was called Isaac, but we haven't heard of anyone called Luke, yet."

"Perhaps there might be some more information about Luke upstairs," suggested Beth, so she and Pip decided to go and have another look in Rose's room.

Nanna thought she would show Gramps the library, and they could have another look at the family tree, to see if there was anyone called Luke in that. She knew the children could find their own way, and Pip and Beth were happy to go off alone.

They had climbed both flights of stairs, and were going along the corridor that led to the bedrooms when they almost bumped into Peter, coming out of one of the rooms. The children were momentarily startled, but he said, in a broad Yorkshire accent, "Now then young 'uns, and have you enjoyed your lunch? It's a grand café they 'ave, 'ere. Did you try them there ice creams? They're to die for!"

Pip couldn't help smiling. Peter just sounded like one of the guys who had lived next door to Nanna and Gramps, years ago, in Yorkshire. "I didn't try an ice cream," he admitted, "But I did have an iced, chocolate coffee, a Mochachino, which was brilliant."

"Well, next time," said Peter, "'ave an ice cream, on the 'ouse of course! Now, don't you forget, Zac said you were to feel free to wander anywhere you like. You can't get lost, so enjoy!" He gave them both a big grin, and headed for the stairs.

They passed the nursery, and glanced in at Isaac's bedroom, on the way, but they soon moved on to Rose's room and pushed the door open. As they entered, Beth felt that things were not quite the same as when they had been there before lunch. The curtains seemed a little wider open, and it was easier to see the things around in the room.

They hadn't noticed before how many bright coloured blankets there were, hanging on the walls, and there was a big blanket box at the end of the bed.

"I never noticed all those, last time," she said.

"It does seem a lot brighter in here, now," said Pip.

"I'm sure things have been moved around," Beth insisted.

They couldn't quite work out what was different, until Beth, who was the more observant, moved over to the side of the bed. She was looking down at the Bible and the photo of Isaac, and she told Pip that she thought they had been moved.

"I'm sure the jewellery box was further back, and the Bible was nearer the bed."

"Come on Beth," he said, "You're getting as bad as me for imagining things," he continued, remembering how he had thought he'd seen a grey figure, in the woods.

Beth picked up the Bible, to put it back where it had been before. It had been carefully slipped into a plastic bag, probably to keep it clean, but as Beth moved it, the Bible began to fall out of the bag. She only just caught it, before it fell in the floor. She was left with an empty plastic bag in her left hand, and the open book in her right. The pages just seemed to flop naturally open at a page that was well used. There were marks down the edges, where someone had repeatedly run their fingers down the side. With her active imagination, Beth looked at a mark where the paper was discoloured in the middle of the page, and she was sure that it was it was made from dried tears.

"Oh, look at this!" she told Pip. "It looks as though someone has been crying."

Pip shook his head. "This whole room feels rather sad," said Pip, "But why would anyone be crying over a book?" he asked, as he walked over to have a look. "Perhaps it's just water that's been spilt."

It was as he was bending down to look at the stain that Pip noticed the name at the top of the page.

"Beth," he exclaimed, "It's Luke!"

"Where?" asked Beth, looking round, half expecting to see someone there.

"No," explained Pip, "In the Bible, the page is open at Luke, it says so at the top!"

Beth looked down, and sure enough the Bible had fallen open at the Gospel of Luke.

"You're right!" she said. Then she thought about the letters they had been looking at over lunch. "Just a minute," she continued, "If the Luke on the sampler isn't a person, but part of the Bible, I wonder if the numbers are something to do with this page."

Nanna had been teaching the children how to find references in the new Bibles they had just bought.

"Let's have a look at your paper again!" said Pip.

Beth was already pulling it out of her bag. Soon they were both looking at the list again.

I O 9 8 7 6 5 4 3 2 1 S A A C L U K E 1 9 V 8 4 M E

"Do you think it could be?" she asked, excitedly.

"Well, it looks like Luke chapter 19 to me," said Pip, glancing down at the Bible as he said so. "And this page that it fell open at starts with Luke chapter 18 and goes right through to the beginning of chapter 19."

"It's right in the middle, just where the tears are!" said Beth.

"If they are tears," said Pip, rather sceptically.

"Let's go over to the window," suggested Beth. "It's a bit difficult to see, over here."

She took the Bible and Pip carried the sheet. "The next letter is V," he read, "And Nanna said sometimes people use that instead of writing out the word, 'verse', so that would be verse 84. What does chapter 19 verse 84 say?" he asked, as Beth could see the Bible easier.

"There aren't eighty four verses," she said, "So it can't mean that."

"Oh," said Pip, disappointedly. He thought for a moment, then, "How many verses are there?" he asked.

"Forty eight," she answered, turning over the page to see.

"Do you think she could have made a mistake," he asked, "And got the numbers the wrong way around?"

"What," said Beth, doubtfully, "And spent ages stitching each one. I don't think so!"

"Just a thought," said Pip, secretly agreeing with her. "Well, if it isn't 84 or 48, what about verse 8, what does that say?"

Beth turned back to the page that had fallen open.

"Wow!" she said, immediately. "It's about Zacchaeus. We'll have to tell him!"

"Tell who?" asked Pip, not understanding.

"Tell our Zac, of course!" said Beth. She looked back at the Bible. "This verse is about Zacchaeus and Jesus."

"What does it say?" insisted Pip, trying to see.

"It says, 'But Zacchaeus stood up and said to the Lord, "Look, Lord! Here and now I give half of my possessions to the poor, and if I have cheated anybody out of anything, I will pay back four times the amount.'" she read.

"It does seem to be part of the story of Zacchaeus, doesn't it?" said Pip. "I'm sure Zac will be pleased." He was feeling rather pleased with himself. "Well, now we have somewhere to start with the mystery. Clue number 1 sorted! Let's go tell the others. This is going to be easy!" he added, with enthusiasm.

"Just a minute," said Beth. "Let me put the Bible back in its bag. Do you think . . ." but she didn't get a chance to ask her question, as at that moment Peter called them.

"Nah then, you two," said Peter, popping his head around the door, and exaggerating his Yorkshire accent. "You don't want to be spending all of this luvvly day indoors, do you? Let's be having you!"

"We were just coming," said Pip.

"Can I bring this down?" asked Beth, holding the Bible. "There's something I need to show Zac."

Peter hesitated, but saw that she was keen to bring it. "Well," he began, "These things are supposed to stay in here. In fact, that should be inside its dust cover, shouldn't it?"

Beth suddenly felt a bit guilty about the fact that the Bible had fallen out of its bag. She knew that it was part of Peter's responsibility in the museum, to make sure everything was properly protected.

"I'm s . . . sorry," she stammered.

"We didn't mean to," said Pip, defending Beth, "But we think it's one of the clues."

"Clues?" asked Peter, seeming a little confused. "What clues?"

"To the mystery," answered Beth.

"To the mystery?" repeated Peter, none the wiser. "I know nought about a mystery."

"Well, Zac told us that Rose is a mystery woman," explained Pip.

"No one knows much about her," added Beth, "So we thought we would try to find out."

"And on the sampler," Pip continued, wanting to show how clever they had been, "There is this reference to Luke chapter 19, so we looked in the Bible . . ."

"And now we want to show Zac," interrupted Beth, "So can we please take it downstairs with us?" she asked again.

Peter seemed amused at their enthusiasm now, and suddenly grinned broadly. "Nay, I don't see why not, lass," he said. "After all, Zac said you were to 'ave free run o' t' place. Bring it on down wi' ye."

Beth didn't need any more encouragement; she slipped the Bible and her pad into her bag; however, as she left the room she had a strange feeling that something wasn't quite right, and couldn't help looking over her shoulder.

That night back at the house, after a lovely meal, when the children had shared their find with everyone, Zac was intrigued that the well-used page they had discovered included the account of his namesake. He said that they could have no better bedtime story than the one that seemed to mean something special to Rose. So here they were again, sitting on the porch as Zac began.

"He gently moved the leaves to one side," said the cowboy, "So that he could look down at the crowd below. He was too small to see over their heads so he had decided that he would have to climb the tree. It had been difficult; the bark was rough under his fingers, and one or two people had laughed at him, a grown man, clambering up in the branches, but you see, something told him that it was very important for him to listen to the speaker that day . . ."[2]

5

Indians in the Forest

The next morning, although Pip was able to sleep in, Beth found herself waking very early. She remembered Pip saying that he had read from his new Bible, so she quietly opened hers, which she had placed on the bedside-table when she had unpacked. Hers was a beautiful deep red colour; Nanna called it burgundy, and like Pip's the edge of each page was coated in gold. She thought she would find last night's story from Luke, and was soon reading the account.

She lay back on her pillow, and started drifting off to sleep again, but the image of Zacchaeus looking down through the leaves stayed with her. She woke up with a start from a dream where someone was looking through the trees of the forest, watching her. In those moments before the dream disappeared she had the impression of a gray shadow, just like Pip said he had seen yesterday.

Sometime later, after travelling for more than three quarters of an hour through the forest which just seemed to get thicker and thicker as the road turned corner after corner, they eventually drew up outside a small two-storey house. It was in a clearing in the woods. The trees had been felled to make room for the house, but instead of being surrounded by fir trees, it was now set in the middle of a clutter of outbuildings of all manner of different sizes and shapes.

There were a couple of typical American barns, painted red and almost the shape of Dutch barns at home. There was a square stable, a cylindrical water tower, a small generator hut, two larger sheds, a garage and, seeming to be quite out of place, in the middle of a small grassy area, there was a white Indian tipi. As the pick-up truck drew to a halt in the driveway the door of the house was opened by the most enormous woman Pip and Beth had ever seen. She was enveloped in a bright, shocking pink dress, trimmed with vivid lime green. Over it she wore a large, crisp white apron with flowers embroidered all over it. As they jumped out of the truck she opened her arms wide and waited.

Pip and Beth exchanged one of their secret glances, but Zac seemed to guess its meaning, for he said, "If you think that you can get away without a bear-hug from 'Dancing Spring' when you visit her home then you'll be mistaken!"

With that he bounded up the last few steps and was soon wrapped in her embrace as he and Dancing Spring giggled and clapped each other on the back.

"So here are the Treasure Hunters, at last," she said, looking across to Pip and Beth, "And very welcome you are to my humble home." She opened her arms wide again, and both children chose to walk up together, but there was plenty of room in her ample arms for them both to be enfolded in the traditional bear-hug.

They found that after such a beginning there was nothing formal about their visit to the Indians in the forest. They were soon sitting out in the afternoon sunshine drinking homemade lemonade from an assorted collection of brightly coloured and differently shaped plastic cups. The lemonade was fresh and tangy, juicy and full of ice cubes; slices of lemon, orange and limes pierced by those bright paper umbrellas floated in the tops of their drinks. Piled onto a red plastic tray were some of the biggest homemade biscuits Pip had ever seen.

"Help yourselves to some cookies!" encouraged Dancing Spring. "Once Grey Wolf comes home they won't last long."

The children, and even Zac didn't need to be asked again, Zac explaining that Dancing Spring's cookies were famous throughout northern Oregon. Pip chose a double chocolate creation that had the moistest chocolate middle he'd ever tasted and Beth went for a chunky ginger biscuit with pieces of real ginger and nuggets of rich dark chocolate folded into it. Zac's choice was one that he always had when he came to visit, with oatmeal, honey and roasted almonds.

Dancing Spring was quick to point out that she and Grey Wolf were members of the Black Foot tribe, and preferred to be called First Nations people or Native Americans, rather than Indians. She explained that in the fifteenth century Christopher Columbus had thought that he had discovered a new route to the continent of India, and so called the Natives 'Indians'.

"These days most First Nations people live on the reservations, their own tribal lands, but when Grey Wolf left the ways of the ancestors, we moved from the reservation to make our own encampment here in the forest. At first I missed the community of the tribe, but gradually the tribal members began to call in here on their way through the woods, some of them even staying for a few days. You'll have seen the tipi we have erected out in the clearing. We put it there to show them that they are always welcome. Don't worry," she added, "That's not the one we're lending you for the week. You are going to use my own special tipi. I don't know if Zac told you, but I am a princess of the Black Foot tribe." She looked across at Zac, who shook his head. "My tipi bears the identification marks of my father and grandfather, as chiefs of the tribe. Come and see!"

She took them over to the largest of the outhouses. It was dim inside, but as she and Zac each drew one of the heavy wooden doors aside the sunlight flooded in, showing an extravagance of colour; every shade of the rainbow was represented among the rows and rows of coat hangers, filled with all sorts of clothing, which lined the sides of the barn. The central space in the barn didn't have floorboards, but was covered with grass. It contained what Pip and Beth assumed was a log pile.

Dancing Spring took them to the far corner where she clambered on top of a small cart, which was almost hidden beneath a pile of boxes and chests, most of which were open and spilling their multicoloured rolls of fabric over every conceivable surface. She brushed these aside, and instead began pulling out a huge piece of principally white canvas, that had bright geometrical designs covering the lower half of it.

"This is the tipi cover which I inherited from my family," she explained, as Zac gave her a hand and they pulled and tugged at the strong material, until they finally had it laid out on the barn floor.

"These are the mountains of our ancestral homeland," she said, indicating the bright blue and purple triangles that covered the bottom of the canvas. There were yellow stars above, and a large yellow sun. "And this is our family emblem," she pointed to the skull of a buffalo, depicted very realistically in grey, red and white on a bright turquoise square of cloth. "It occurs here and here," she said, pointing again, to other parts of the canvas, where the design of the buffalo was repeated a number of times, and finally showing them that a larger version of it was used to decorate the flap which would cover the door.

Pip and Beth looked in amazement at the sheer length of the canvas; it seemed huge. Above the mountains they could just make out the golden rays of the sun.

"Wow!" said Pip, "It's brilliant!"

"It's much better than the one outside in your garden," said Beth. "Are you sure you don't mind us borrowing it?"

"It is my pleasure," answered Dancing Spring. "Never have any of my tribe been host to the White People from over the Great Water. It is an honour for my family. For hundreds of years we have heard the stories of your people, and now finally to meet you, and to know that you are to sleep beneath the ancient canvas is satisfaction enough. You are welcome!" She looked over at Zac, and added, "And the Davidsons have done so much for the tribes over the years that we are happy to do anything we can for your guests of honour."

Pip and Beth smiled; they were really looking forward to their week sleeping in the tipi.

Then came the rather long job of folding up the canvas again, which took the four of them about twenty minutes to achieve. Finally it was in a bundle small enough to fill the back of the pick-up truck.

"Now, before we pack the tipi poles," said Dancing Spring, indicating the pile of logs which the children had thought was firewood, "You must receive your gifts."

"Our gifts?" asked the children in unison.

"But of course," said Dancing Spring, "Surely Zac has explained that if you are going to be part of the Rendezvous, you must live as we did in 1840, so you cannot wear your ordinary clothing; and, after all, dressmaking is something that I know all about," she said, flinging her arms around in an expansive gesture which seemed to include all the racks of clothes in the barn.

First she reached a couple of coat hangers down, which had long dresses on them. She held out a dark blue and green checked dress towards Beth. It was made of quite thick material and had long sleeves.

"Even in the height of summer, the evenings come in very cold," she said. "You will be glad of the warmth of this, and we'll choose you both some blankets and ponchos to wear of an evening around the campfire. But July can have soaring temperatures during the day," she continued, displaying the second dress for them to see. It was made of pink and black pinstriped cotton, with white lace around the neck and the bottom of the short sleeves. "This will be ideal. I had your grandparents send over your measurements, and there are bags over in the house with some things for them to borrow, too, but I would like you two to accept these as our gifts, for you to take home to remember your encampment at the Rendezvous." She reached into one of the wooden chests and brought out a large white apron, similar to, but a little smaller than, the one she wore. "Of course," she added, "Life on the encampment isn't just fun, there will be lots of chores to be done, and you won't want to get your dresses marked."

Beth was really pleased with her gifts, but Pip was a bit apprehensive about what he would get. He wasn't too sure about the two handmade shirts Dancing Spring passed off the rack. One wasn't too bad, it was dark blue with tiny white spots all over it, but the other was dark red with little pale green leaves covering it. They both had huge full sleeves, caught into broad cuffs, and they had open necks with leather laces at the front.

"You'll probably prefer your own trousers," continued Dancing Spring, much to his relief, glancing down at his jeans. "They are quite authentic for the period, for the guys anyway," she added, looking at Beth's blue jeans. "No self respecting woman would be seen dead in jeans in the 1840's!"

"Thanks," said Pip, as she passed him a beautifully tooled leather belt.

"And of course," added Dancing Spring, reaching into a large leather bag, "We have moccasins for you all."

Beth's and Nanna's moccasins were the kind both children had been expecting, rather like the suede slippers you get in England, but these had beadwork sewn on the tops, in turquoise, black and white. As she popped them on, Beth thought how long it must have taken to sew each bead on individually.

Pip's and Gramps' however were quite different; the foot part was nearly the same, but with no decoration (which Pip was really pleased about) but attached to them was more of the beautiful soft tan leather, making them into boots.

"You wear them over your trousers, and lace them like this," explained Dancing Spring, bending to show him how the leather thongs crossed backwards and forwards around his legs, making a snug fit.

"They're so comfy I hardly feel I am wearing any shoes at all!" he said.

Dancing Spring simply smiled, and then said, "And finally!"

She drew the children over to the other side of the barn, where a worktable was set up, covered with all sorts of leather tools and clothing. She reached over and passed them a jacket each, made of the finest tan leather, with long fringes on the shoulders and intricate beadwork all down the front and back.

The children were amazed. They could tell that they would be worth a small fortune in a shop. They were wonderful, Pip even liked the patterns on these; they were geometrical, black, white and red.

"You are our honoured guests," said Dancing Spring. "Grey Wolf has spent many hours preparing for your trip," she said. "He should be home soon. He is known as a great craftsman; he is very skilled at leather working."

"They have obviously been made with you in mind," said Zac, "Look at this!" he pointed to the design on the back of the jacket he was holding. It depicted a fish, a box and an open book.

"The treasure you found in your own country!" explained Dancing Spring. "Zac has been telling us all about your adventures as Treasure Hunters."

Pip smiled, he still found it hard to believe how many people were interested in their discovery, last year, of the treasure of Crickley Manor. It had almost made them famous, even here in America.

The early evening shadows were lengthening as the last of the poles were tied down onto the pick-up truck, with long ropes holding them firmly in place. The temperature took quite a sudden drop and as Beth looked over at the nearest trees of the forest she realised that a mist was drifting in. There were wispy strands of white clouds making the trees seem more distant than before. Suddenly she remembered her dream of the morning, the dream about a gray figure watching through the trees. She began gently rubbing the tops of her arms; it was quite cool standing there peering into the forest.

Pip followed the direction of Beth's gaze, and they both felt the hairs on the back of their necks begin to rise, as they heard a mournful howl far off in the woods.

"At last, Grey Wolf is home!" said Dancing Spring; she turned to see the area of forest they were looking at.

Even as they watched, the dusk was deepening and Beth became aware of the outline of a grey figure moving out of the woods towards them. She took a step closer to Pip, as they waited. Soon they could all make out the shaggy outline of a man dressed all in grey, from his head down to his long grey moccasins. His hair was grey, his clothes and even the old blanket that covered the pack that he was carrying over his shoulder was grey. A lean, grey dog was loping along at his side.

As the two figures came towards them the animal drew back his lips and bared his teeth, menacingly. Pip gasped and shuddered as he realised it wasn't a dog at all.

It was a wolf.

6

Under the Stars

Grey Wolf came to a halt just in front of them. Zac smiled at him, but did not attempt to shake hands, as he had with everyone else they had met on their trip. Instead he kept his hands by his side, and just nodded, "Hello," in Grey Wolf's direction, and the Indian nodded silently back.

"Our guests," said Dancing Spring, "Pip and Beth, from the Old Country," she indicated the children.

"Huh," grunted Grey Wolf.

"We need to be leaving, before the mist deepens," said Zac, moving towards the pick-up.

"Huh," repeated Grey Wolf, looking down the road, in the direction they would be going. "Dark soon!" he said; then he looked straight at Pip. "You, take care!" he added, his piercing grey eyes boring into Pip's.

"Err, yes!" said Pip, feeling more uncomfortable than he had all day.

"And, err, thank you for the clothes," said Beth to Dancing Spring, who seemed to have gone awfully quiet, now that her husband was home.

"Yes, thanks," said Pip, glad that Zac was already getting into the pick-up, and that they would soon be leaving.

"Huh," said Grey Wolf, raising his hand in farewell.

"Will we see you at the Rendezvous?" asked Zac, as he started up the engine.

Dancing Spring looked over at her husband, who remained silent. "It may be that you will," she said, waving as they drew off down the drive and onto the long forest road home. Pip had thought that she had seemed so warm and friendly, such a contrast to Grey Wolf. Pip glanced out of the rear window. Grey Wolf was just standing staring after the departing truck, the wolf at his feet. Pip could almost feel his eyes following them down the road.

He dug his elbow into Beth, whispering, "That was a bit weird. He was so quiet, and a bit scary, wasn't he?"

"Yes," she whispered back, "And what about that wolf, it was a bit of a strange pet to have."

"I know what you mean. I wouldn't like to meet him alone in the woods on a dark night." Pip shivered.

The children were quite hungry when they arrived back at the house, and it was beginning to get quite dark. They were glad that Bella May had fixed up some simple sandwiches, which they all ate around the kitchen table. Bella May had been telling them how the tent that she, Timothy and Zac would be using was like a little house, with a huge stove inside.

"On a night like tonight," she said, "It's so nice to sit around the stove, and tell stories."

"And on that suggestion," added Zac, "How about our bedtime story?"

Beth rested her head on her hands, and Pip leaned back, and crossed his feet. He was really enjoying this part of the holiday.

So Zac began. "The new coat was exactly the right size. As he twisted and turned, the fabric seemed to have every colour of the rainbow."[3]

Beth lifted her head and looked at Pip. She was remembering all those bright coloured fabrics they had seen, earlier that day. He winked, and of course they both recognised the story.

"When his brothers looked at him, they were filled with envy," Zac continued, and they all enjoyed his version of the story of Joseph.

It was a glorious, sunny evening when they arrived to set up the tipi at the Rendezvous. They had spent most of the day in final preparations for this week's encampment. They had collected all the items from the museum that they would be using to help everything to be authentic, just as it would have been in the 1840's. Those things were now neatly stacked in the hallway of the museum, ready to be carried over to the tents later. They had then gone back to the house for their costumes and the tipi itself.

Pip and Beth had thought that as the Rendezvous was being held in the grounds of the museum it would just be like camping out in the garden. How wrong they were!

By the time Zac parked their pick-up on the front lawn of the museum the whole place had changed. There were already half a dozen tents erected. These were not tipis, but were the square, white 'miners' tents, like the one Timothy and Bella May had. These looked like little white houses, with four straight walls, a ridged roof and even a chimney at the back.

Pip looked around the lawn, and saw that three of the tents seemed to house families, whereas the others appeared to be stalls, selling a variety of different things. One was full of leather goods, jackets with fringes on them (much simpler than the ones they had), belts, bags and shoes. Another tent was full of sweets and biscuits, 'candy and cookies' the Americans would call them, he thought. The third trader was hung with every imaginable piece of bead-jewellery; necklaces, broaches, rings, bracelets, anklets and even thin strips of leather and beads for you to make up your own designs. They would have plenty to investigate in a little while, but first they had to help erect the tipi.

They neither of them liked helping to put the tent up when they were camping with Mum and Dad, but this was going to be different. They eagerly set about unloading the wooden poles from the truck. Zac and Gramps could just manage one each, but Pip and Beth carried one between them, Pip taking the heavy end, and Beth, about twelve feet in front of him, carrying the tapered point each time.

When they had been loading the poles onto the pick-up Dancing Spring had pointed out that three of them were much longer than the other nine. She had called them the 'key poles'. As they now unloaded all the poles onto the lawn, they quickly identified these 'key poles' again. One of them was the longest of all. "King pin," said Zac.

"But we need the other two first," he added, as he took a short length of rope out of his pocket.

"Is that all the rope we are going to need?" asked Gramps, surprised. He was thinking of how long the guy ropes were for an ordinary tent back home.

"It is," smiled Zac. "It's the only bit of rope that a tipi needs to hold the whole thing up. Just watch and see!"

They walked over the lawn to the spot they had chosen to erect their tipi, carrying the three 'key poles' with them. Zac asked Pip and Beth to take hold of the two posts he needed first. They let the heavy ends stay on the floor, and picked up each pole by its centre. Zac brought the two tapered ends together, holding them at about waist-height. The children could see that a shallow groove had been scored around them both, about a metre from the end, and they watched as Zac began to bind them together with the rope.

"Ready!" he said, in a moment or two, as he finished off the knot. He and Gramps went to the heavy ends of these poles.

"We need to make them into an 'A' frame," he explained to the children. "We'll open them wide at the bottom, and then if you two would like to support their bases for a while, your Gramps and I will do the heavy construction."

Zac positioned Pip at the edge of an imaginary circle, which he indicated with his hands.

"We'll pitch it here," he said. "If you and Gramps will hold this one, Beth and I will move the other one." Zac then paced out twelve strides, taking Beth to another point on the imaginary circle.

"Now then," he said, "If Gramps and I gently lift these two poles, then you two can keep standing at the base to give it a bit of support."

Next Zac brought over the 'king-pin', the longest of all the tipi poles.

"Whoops," he said, smiling, "I almost forgot! This needs to be attached to the canvas, first! Are you two OK for a minute or two?"

They assured him that they were. In fact they both found that because the heavy poles were resting on each other, their job was really quite easy.

Zac and Gramps now had to drag the heavy canvas from the pick-up truck down onto the ground. They dragged it over the lawn, while the children watched. Dancing Spring had made sure that the lacing at the top of the canvas was easily visible, and Zac soon found it. He simply tied it around another knife groove in the top of the 'king-pin'.

"Now we are ready," he said. Again he paced out twelve strides, until he was equidistant from both Pip and Beth. He carefully placed the base of the 'king-pin' there, again on his imaginary circle, and then he and Gramps began to raise the 'king-pin' with the canvas attached high above their heads. When it was almost upright they gently lowered its thin end, where the canvas had been tied, until it rested on the roped section where the children's poles were joined together. For the moment the canvas was hanging straight down in the centre of the poles. The whole structure now outlined three sides of a triangular pyramid.

"That's the technical bit over," Zac said. "Now for the heavy lifting!"

He and Gramps then placed the other nine poles over the three key poles; three went on each side of the pyramid. Zac pulled the bottoms of the poles out slightly, to form the circle, their tops crossing one another above the canvas. Next each pole was stood upright and then gently lowered to rest where the key poles met. Soon Pip and Beth could clearly see the skeleton of the tipi. Zac told the children they could let go, now; the poles were supporting each other perfectly.

The canvas was still just hanging down from the 'king-pin'. Zac drew it out between two of the poles and then began to unwind it, walking slowly around the edge of the poles. Soon the canvas covered all the poles, overlapping at the door, and in only a minute or two, the tipi was 'dressed' in all its finery. Pip and Beth took a moment or two to simply gaze at the striking designs of sun, mountains and buffalo skulls that they had glimpsed in Dancing Spring's barn. It really was a magnificent sight.

"It's much better than the other white tents," said Beth. "I'm so glad that Dancing Spring lent us this one. It seems so much more . . . Indian!"

"First Nations!" Pip corrected her, laughing, but he was equally impressed. "Just look at those buffalo skulls; they look so real, with the red and white feathers painted underneath them. They look scary enough to frighten away any enemies!"

Once the canvas had been placed, the 'smoke flaps' were erected. The children knew that they wouldn't be having a fire in their tipi, but of course First Nations people lived in their tipis all year round, so they would need a fire. These smoke flaps were a simple design, which covered the upper part of the canvas. They were attached to two other smaller wooden poles, which fitted into two pouches. In winter they would be opened to allow the smoke from a central fire to escape through a hole at the top of the tipi. In summer the smoke flaps could be adjusted to make the opening at the top much wider, to let fresh air inside. Finally the door panel was attached; it was an oblong piece of canvas with a larger version of the buffalo skull painted on it, looking most dramatic.

Pip pushed the panel to one side, and was the first to enter the tipi. They were amazed at how big it was inside. Their lounge at home was about sixteen feet long, and Gramps said that the tipi was at least as wide across as that. It was almost a circle, and they had decided that Nanna and Gramps would have the right-hand side of the tipi as their room, and the children would have the other side.

It was now time to collect the extra things from the museum. Gramps helped Zac to pull the old wooden blanket box they had taken from the museum inside their tipi.

"Nothing better than these to keep you warm at night," Zac said.

Gramps smiled, and opened the box and they brought out one after another of the beautiful, handcrafted Indian blankets of the most amazing designs. When more than a dozen were strewn around the tipi floor they began to choose which ones they wanted to cover their beds. Pip chose a bright green one, with black and white chessboard edging as the one to cover all the others on his bed. Beth's choice was in rich browns, reds, and oranges, and made her feel warm just by looking at it. Nanna and Gramps covered their bed with a turquoise and pink striped blanket which looked really bright over in their half of the tipi.

It didn't take Gramps long to rig up a rope line across the middle of the tent, and he hung a couple more of the Indian blankets at both sides to make brightly coloured bedroom walls, separating the two bedroom areas.

The old foam mattresses, which Bella May had insisted that they brought along, were soon laid in place; Nanna and Gramps put theirs together to make a double bed, and Pip and Beth placed theirs end to end. They had decided to put the pillow ends together, so that they could chat quietly late into the night.

Their cases full of clothes made good bedside tables, to keep their books, torches and drinks on. They were covered with small mats during the day, so that visitors to the Rendezvous, who would have access to wander around as they pleased, would see nothing modern. All that remained to be done was cover the short grass inside the tipi with even more of the Indian blankets. They left the few spare blankets inside the box, which they put right in the middle of the tent, as a centrepiece.

Sitting around the stove that night, in Zac's tent, it was Bella May who chose to tell the story of the wise and foolish builders.[4] She smiled as she reminded them, "We've all kind of been building houses, today, so I thought this would be a good story."

They all laughed at her description of the fall of the house built on sand. While she had been telling the story, Timothy had been boiling the water to make hot-water bottles. He opened the front of the fire, to let some heat out.

"You could make a nice bit of toast on that," said Gramps, with a wink.

"We often do," answered Timothy.

"Oh, but I didn't bring our toasting fork, this time," confessed Bella May.

Suddenly Pip remembered seeing the long toasting fork beside the fireplace in the hall of the museum, and suggested borrowing it.

At that moment Peter from the museum popped his head round the door, asking if they were all settling in; he had brought his camper van onto the Rendezvous. When he heard about Pip's suggestion of the toasting fork from the museum, he offered to go along and unlock the door for him.

They chatted along the short walk to the museum, Peter asking how they were getting on with the mystery and about all the things that were planned for the next few days. He told Pip that on the 5th of

July, the day after the Museum's Anniversary Parade, there was going to be a special celebration at Fort Clatsop.

"'Ave you seen the film 'Night in t' Museum'?" he asked.

Pip smiled; it was one of their Dad's favourites, Mum had bought it for Christmas, and they'd all enjoyed watching it time and time again, laughing at all the fun.

"You bet!" he answered.

"Well," went on Peter, "You'll remember the beautiful Indian girl, Sacagawea." Pip nodded; she was one of Beth's favourite characters.

"At the Fort," Peter continued, "They 'ave some of her clothes and things on display, and this year they're goin' to enact part of the story. I fancy goin' meself, and I wondered if you two'd like to come along. We can check it out with your grandparents, and then I'll take you, if you like."

Pip thought it would be interesting, and he was sure that Beth would want to go, too, and they arranged that Peter would pick them up in the morning of the day after Independence Day. They had now arrived at the museum, and Peter unlocked the door, letting Pip go inside for the fork. Pip crossed the hall and made straight for the fireplace.

He bent down to pick up the fork, and as he was straightening up again, his eyes rested on the wording under the huge, brass clock, and his heart suddenly missed a beat. Why hadn't he noticed that before? The words were in Latin, 'Tempus Fugit' and weren't they the words on the sampler? Suppose there was something here at the fireside for them to find?

He was just thinking about this, when he heard a slight noise behind him. He turned and saw that it was only Peter, who was leaning casually on the doorframe, but he seemed to be intently watching Pip. Pip decided that he wouldn't say anything about his find just yet. He waved the toasting fork in the air and shouted, "Got it!"

He decided that tomorrow he would find an excuse to come into the museum again, but without an audience. At least now he had an idea that the clock was part of the mystery.

That first night in the tipi felt really rather cosy, as they lay beneath their Indian blankets, snug and warm, but still able to see the stars shining above through the smoke flaps which pulled wide open, to let in the night air.

Soon the chatter from Nanna and Gramps' side of the tipi died down, and Pip whispered to Beth about the words on the clock. Because she had written the clue into her book, she remembered the poem being about a mother and son. She remembered the first time that she looked at the clock; at that time she hadn't realised that most of the things in the museum were about Rose and Isaac, but now as she thought about the words 'mother and son', the image of a young mother showing a flower to her toddler came back to her.

She described it to Pip. "And of course, she was holding a banjo!" she finished with, remembering the words of the sampler:

> Where mother and son
> Stoop to admire it
> Banjo is playing
> Tempus Fugit.

The children could hardly wait until the morning to check it out. Then all thought of the morning vanished as they heard again the sound of a wolf howling in the nearby forest. A strange feeling crept over them. What if they were really being watched? What if this mystery was more dangerous than they thought? What if . . . ?

7

The Search

The following morning there was no time to revisit the museum; there was so much to do. Between their tipi and Zac's, Timothy and his father had dug a fire pit, erected the cooking irons, and covered the whole area with a canopy. By the time Pip and Beth were up and dressed in their Rendezvous clothes a fire was burning in the pit, and the large metal kettle, which was hanging from the central iron above the fire, was sending steam into the air.

"You're just in time," Zac greeted them, "We're just about to make breakfast: biscuits and gravy."

Pip glanced over to Beth, and was just in time to see the look of horror on her face, before she struggled to smile at Zac.

"Surely we can't have heard correctly," she whispered to Pip, a moment later, when the grown-ups were not listening. "What can he mean, 'biscuits and gravy'?" she asked.

"Well," answered Pip "The only picture that comes into my mind is a plateful of sweet biscuits, like digestives, or chocolate cookies, with the thick, dark brown gravy that we have on Sundays with our Yorkshire puddings for dinner."

"Ugh!" said Beth, unable to keep the disgust out of her voice. "Is that what people had to eat in the 1840s?" she asked, adding, "How awful!"

"Awful?" questioned Zac, having caught her last word. "Don't you like biscuits and gravy? I thought it was everyone's favourite."

Nanna was just coming out of the tent, and had heard what was being said. She too was not sure exactly what they were going to be eating, but felt that they should give it a try. After all, they had enjoyed everything else they had eaten over here.

"Actually," she began, "I don't think we've ever had biscuits in gravy before."

"Never had biscuits and gravy?" asked Zac, in amazement. "But that's a shame; you're in for a treat today."

Gramps wandered over from one of the stalls, where he had been chatting to the traders, and said, "Well, I, for one, am really looking forward to outdoor cooking. I love barbequing at home, but this system looks really impressive, cooking over open flames."

At that moment, Bella May and Timothy came over, with their arms full of wooden stools, and soon everyone was seated around the fire-pit, as Timothy and Zac set about the cooking. Timothy explained that he was going to make the biscuits in the Dutch oven. This was a large, heavy metal pot, with a tight fitting lid. He put this directly onto the coals, at one side of the fire. While the pot was heating up, he brought out some dough, which he had made earlier, and left to rise. He now rolled the dough into balls, about the size of golf balls. When he had a couple of dozen of these, he carefully opened the Dutch oven, and filled the bottom with the dough balls, brushed the top of them with a little milk, and then firmly covered them with the lid.

"Not long now," he said, looking over at Zac, who had a big, heavy open frying pan heating at the other side of the fire.

Zac opened the cool box and soon there was a sizzling noise, as sausage meat dropped onto the hot metal.

"Sausage?" asked Pip, his eyes lighting up. Sausage was one of his favourites.

The appetizing smell was soon filling the air, and drawing one or two of the traders over to watch.

"Biscuits and gravy on your first morning!" exclaimed the lady from the bead tent. "My, you are lucky, we only had time for coffee, this morning."

Bella May grinned. "You know what Dad's like for his breakfast," she said.

Pip and Beth found that their appetite was coming back, now. They watched, as Zac simply added a little flour, milk and water to his pan, and soon had a lovely, creamy sauce, with chunks of sausage meat bubbling in his pan. Timothy looked at his watch, and took hold of a thick oven glove to raise the lid of the oven. Now to add to the smell of sausages, the scent of freshly made bread greeted them all.

Beth was the nearest, and bent forward to have a look inside the oven.

"Wow!" she said, looking into the pot. The little 'golf balls' of dough had risen and expanded. When Timothy began to get them out, they could all see the golden brown 'biscuits'. When they opened them on their enamel plates they were all soft inside.

"Why, they are almost like scones," said Nanna.

Zac showed them how to tear the biscuits open, and then he poured the rich sausage gravy over the top, and passed round the forks. Pip and Beth both said afterwards, they didn't remember enjoying such a wonderful breakfast before.

"There's nothing like eating outside," said Gramps, helping himself to another biscuit.

"You're right!" said Zac, passing round the strawberry jam, which he called strawberry jelly. There was no gravy left. "We can't leave these last few biscuits, can we?" he asked. The children didn't need any more encouragement, and were soon eating the soft, doughy biscuits, with huge fruity strawberries on top.

"Well," said Pip, "Biscuits and gravy turned out to be nothing like I imagined." When he explained, the Americans laughed.

"There's no wonder you looked so horrified, when I first told you," said Zac, smiling over at Beth. "Cookies with meat sauce, how horrible. Ugh!" he said, doing a good imitation of Beth's face, when she first heard what was for breakfast. She chuckled.

"We don't just need an English/American dictionary," said Pip, "We need a cookbook, too!"

Nanna smiled, "Well that would be a good souvenir to take home."

When they began to do the clearing-up after breakfast, the lady from the stall with all the beads and necklaces on invited them to come over and have a closer look at her goods. Nanna and Beth were more than pleased to go, and when Pip realised that it was either that or help Gramps with the washing-up, he went along, too. Although there was a lot to see, the children were most interested in a large wooden bowl at the front of the stall which was filled with all kinds of different beads. There were beads of every colour you could imagine, some metal ones, and glass ones, all in different sizes, some round, some square, some long ones.

Nanna picked up some of them to have a better look; they were almost white and quite smooth; you could tell that they were hand-carved.

"Are these made of ivory?" she asked.

"No, no," said the lady, "They're not ivory. Indians carve these from bone."

"Real bones?" asked Pip, picking one up to examine it more closely.

The lady explained that you could buy a lace made from leather; of whatever length you wanted, and then thread it with your own choice of beads.

"Since you are our honoured guests," she said, smiling, "Would you like to have a go?"

Soon the children were sitting cross-legged, absorbed in their creations. Beth chose lots of bright turquoise and black beads, whereas Pip went for the bone ones and a few of the brass beads. He even found one that looked like the tooth of a wild animal, but found that it was the tip of an antler. Even so it looked quite impressive as the centrepiece of his neckband.

They had almost finished, when Zac came over to see if they wanted a chance to practise with the tomahawks. There was to be a tomahawk throwing competition later, so they went off into a clearing in the woods where the targets had all been set out. They both had fun trying to whirl the small axes through the air at the different pictures on the targets. Pip was much better than Beth, at least his tomahawk occasionally landed on the target. Zac strode over and with a quick twist of the wrist sent the axe whistling across the ground to land with a loud thump right in the middle of the target.

"That's how to throw a tomahawk," he said. "You need to remember that these were used to hunt and kill! You just wait until the First Nations guys are throwing!" said Zac. "Some of them could split a hair with a tomahawk, they're so accurate!"

Pip found he was really looking forward to seeing the competition.

The day had just rushed away with so many new things to see and try. It wasn't until late in the afternoon that Pip and Beth had time to investigate the clock in the museum. By then the opening hours of the museum were over, but Zac lent them his key, told them to let themselves in, and make sure that all the lights were out and the door locked again when they came back for the evening meal in an hour or so. It was getting dark and there were long shadows that seemed to be reaching across the door towards the children.

Pip opened the heavy door, and was about to head straight for the clock, when Beth suggested he lock the door behind them.

"That way we are sure that we won't be disturbed," she said.

"Good idea!" exclaimed Pip. "We will be able to have a better search, with no-one else being around."

With the door firmly locked, they made their way to the fireplace. Beth already had her drawing pad out.

"Look!" said Pip, pointing to the inscription beneath the figures, 'Tempus fugit.'

Beth looked, and nodded. Then she read out the poem from the sampler.

Where mother and son
Stoop to admire it
Banjo is playing
Tempus Fugit.

"Well," said Pip, "There is certainly a mother and son here on the clock."

"But what are they admiring?" asked Beth leaning closer. She remembered the bee from the other day, and as soon as she looked again she remembered the flower. "A wild rose!" she exclaimed. "Perhaps it is something to do with our Rose."

"So we're on the right track!" cried Pip. "On the sampler, I noticed that directly underneath the poem was a picture of a key, but what is she trying to tell us with that?"

"Maybe," mused Beth, "Underneath the clock, there might be a key."

Both children bent to look. The mantelpiece was almost at the right height for Beth to look without bending much at all, and the clock was so big that their heads didn't even come close to knocking into one another as they stooped to look.

"Nothing!" they called out, together.

"Well, just a minute," said Pip, "Rose can't have hidden anything just underneath the clock. It's bound to have been moved over the years."

"Of course," agreed Beth, "You would have to be able to dust under there. It must be hidden somewhere nearby."

They began to look around the rest of the fireplace.

"But the clock might get moved somewhere else," suggested Pip, "So perhaps the clue must mean the key is hidden in the clock itself."

Immediately both children began to examine the clock more closely, Pip at the left hand side and Beth at the right. Pip soon discovered that there was a small drawer on his side, at the base of the clock, with a tiny brass knob.

"Da, da!" he said, opening the drawer and brandishing a small brass key, triumphantly. "I've got it!"

Beth couldn't see a drawer at her side, so she came round to see what he had found.

"Wait a minute," she said, "Nanna and Gramps have a clock which needs to be wound up. Perhaps this one does too. Look, there is a little brass key hole in the middle of the clock face."

"You could be right," said Pip, reluctantly, and when he opened up the glass front of the clock, the little brass key was a perfect fit.

Beth somehow managed not to say 'I told you so', and instead went to have another look at her side of the clock. The base was wooden. She had noticed that the little drawer at Pip's side had a brass rectangle embossed around its edges, and when she looked again at her side, there was the same kind of decoration.

"Why isn't this a drawer, too?" she muttered, running her fingers along it.

"Let me see!" said Pip, closing the clock face, and returning the key to its place. The tension was beginning to get to them.

He tried to push her aside, to get a better look, but she pushed him back. In the struggle that followed he ended up slipping to the floor. She grabbed out at the clock, to stop falling too, pushing hard on the brass rectangle at her side of the clock. Suddenly a concealed drawer simply popped open.

"Wow!" she exclaimed. Pip scrambled up to look as she reached inside to pull out a somewhat larger, silver key. It was attached to a faded tag, which read: "my chest". This silver key was rather tarnished, whereas the brass one that Pip had had was quite shiny.

"I suppose the brass key gets used regularly, to wind the clock up," suggested Beth; "This one might not have been outside the hidden drawer for ages, not since Rose left it there, perhaps a hundred years."

"I wonder which chest it means?" asked Pip. "Never mind how long it has been in the drawer; what does it open? Why has she hidden it here? What could be so important about the chest?"

They began to think, wondering which chest she could have meant.

"There were lots of boxes and chests of drawers in the different rooms when we were looking the other day," began Beth; "Perhaps we have time to search, now?"

Pip looked at his watch. "Yeah, why not," he said. "Zac said we had an hour or so, we could make a start, at any rate!"

"So where shall we start?" asked Beth.

"Well, if it is the key to Rose's chest, let's try in her room, first."

That seemed the best idea, so they began to go straight upstairs. Pip ran ahead, taking the stairs two at a time. He was soon running along the corridor to the bottom of the staircase that would take them to the floor where the bedrooms were. Beth was just coming along the darker part of the landing, halfway up the first flight of steps, when she thought she heard the front door close. She thought it must be Zac, coming to get them for supper, so she turned round and called, "Zac, is that you?" but there was no reply.

"Zac?" she called again, retracing her steps, but when she was low enough to be able to see the front door, there was no one in sight.

'I must have been mistaken,' she thought, and ran back to catch up with Pip.

By the time she came through the door Pip had gone straight over to the bedside table, but the small jewel box had no lock.

"We'll try the chest of drawers near the sampler," he suggested, but they could both see that the keyhole was much too small for the key Beth was holding.

"And anyway," she said, pulling the top drawer open, to reveal piles of hand embroidered pillow cases, "Drawers aren't usually called chests!"

"They might have been, years ago," insisted Pip, "And anyway, there is nowhere else in here that might be locked. Perhaps we had better separate. It's nearly time for supper. You could go down the main stairs and check the rooms at the front of the house for any likely chests, and I'll use the back stairs, the ones the servants used to use and check the other rooms. We'll meet at the front door in twenty minutes, OK?"

"OK," she answered, as she turned out of Rose's room and went into the nursery. There were lots of boxes and chests of toys in here, but most of them had their lids propped open to display the toys inside them, and the ones that were closed didn't have locks anyway. She heard Pip coming out of Isaac's room.

"Anything?" she called.

"Nothing yet," he answered, "I'm just off up to the attics. I'll be quick," he added. "The back stairs are easy to find from there. I'll meet you down at the front door. Don't be too long!"

"I won't!" she called after his already disappearing figure.

Now that she was on her own a shudder crept up her back. She had a strange feeling that they were not alone, she glanced over her shoulder. All was quiet and in the distance she could even hear the clock ticking.

8

Hide!

Beth hadn't expected Pip to go up to the creepy attics by himself. She was glad she was searching the front of the house, she wouldn't have liked to go up there alone. As it was she thought she heard a noise behind her, as she was coming along the corridor near the dining room. It was a little bit eerie, being in the museum, alone, and it didn't help that Pip had been talking yesterday about one of their favourite films, 'Night in the museum', where everything comes alive at night. She hurried down the passage into the next room.

It was the ballroom. Today it seemed huge, with its high ceiling and empty wooden floor, which echoed with her every step. She walked towards the lifelike dummies of Rose and Isaac, and as she paused to look at the Christmas tree near where they were standing the noise of her own footsteps stopped and this time she was sure she heard soft footsteps, coming down the hallway she had just left. She knew it couldn't be Pip; he had gone up the attic stairs, in the other direction entirely. Who could it be? All of a sudden Beth knew she didn't want to be found in here all by herself.

She took a quick look around for a hiding place. Apart from the dummies of Isaac and Rose in their Christmas Ball outfits, there wasn't much else in the room. The creak of a floorboard just outside the door caused her to seek shelter in the only available place—underneath Rose's crinoline ball gown.

She had no sooner crept on hands and knees beneath the folds of the yellow skirt, than someone really did walk into the room. Beth had half expected no one would be there, just her own imagination, but she could clearly hear someone walking quietly around. She had made herself into a tight ball at the back of the dummy. She didn't know how long she crouched there, but the back of her legs began to hurt, in their cramped position. All seemed to be quiet in the ballroom, now. Her head was quite near the hem of the dress, so she tried to peer under the skirt.

The footsteps started again, making their way straight towards her. The hair on the back of her neck prickled. She froze. Her left leg began to tremble slightly, under the pressure. The steps stopped, right by the side of the dummy. Then she saw the feet. They were encased in grey moccasins. Her heart skipped a beat. An Indian had been following her, an Indian dressed in grey! The thought terrified her. She was sure he must be able to hear her breathing, and was certain that her heart was pounding loud enough for Pip to hear in the attic.

Just as she was thinking about Pip, she heard him calling, his voice drifting across the room. He must have finished at the top of the house, because his voice came to her from downstairs in the entrance hall.

"Beth, come on, we'll be late if we don't leave now!"

The moment Pip began to call, the intruder turned and ran silently from the room. After a few agonising seconds Beth crawled out from under the ball dress and headed towards the front stairs, and Pip's welcome company. She rubbed her aching calves, as she went.

Pip was already unlocking the front door.

"Let's get out, quick!" she said, to his surprise, and began to tell him all about being followed, as they made their way to the tipi.

He caught hold of her hand as she finished. "Let's go back and see who it was!" he said.

"No!" said Beth, insistently. Whoever it was, and she felt she had a good idea who it had been, they would be long gone by now; and she certainly didn't think they should tackle him alone. "We don't want to be in trouble for being late," she said.

Pip hesitated. "I suppose not," he conceded, "But who do you think . . ." he stopped, as the most likely answer occurred to him. He just stared at Beth, and whispered, "Wow!" under his breath. "What could he want?" he murmured.

The embers of the cooking fire were still glowing red, smoldering gently in the pit when they had all finished another wonderful meal. Zac reached over for another log. Usually at this time of night, as the sun was beginning to set, they let the fire go out, but Pip was sure that Zac deliberately chose the largest log on the pile, one with lots of small branches attached, and one big enough to burn long into the night.

"Anyone for a sing-song?' called Zac, over his shoulder, as he settled the wood in the centre of the fire. Soon there were flames leaping up the smaller branches, crackling and sending sparks into the night air, and just as quickly it seemed to Pip and Beth everyone on the Rendezvous was gathering around their encampment.

A couple of guys had guitars slung over their shoulders and one of the ladies was holding a flute, and of course there were lots of the Indian drums passed around for anyone who wanted to join in. Pip found himself with a small hand-held upright drum; whereas Beth was sitting next to Bella May with the huge pow-wow drum between them. They both had drumsticks for it.

As she looked across the campfire Beth could see so many people, some sitting on chairs, others on rugs on the ground and still others standing in groups, all smiling and joining in as Zac struck up a popular old American folksong, 'Oh Susanna, don't you cry for me'.

The singsong did indeed go on well into the night. The children really enjoyed it, many of the songs were new to them, but they were usually easy to pick up. Often people would explain where the songs had come from, telling stories of long ago. Pip was surprised that lots of the songs described events in the Bible, whilst others told the stories of the early pioneers.

Zac smiled at him. "Many of our ancestors came here because they wanted to build a new life based on their faith. Some of them had been persecuted in their old countries," he said. "But now I think it's time for our bedtime story."

"Go for it, Zac," said the lady who had the leather goods stall.

The children were quite surprised to see everyone put down their instruments, and settle down to hear Zac's story.

"Well, now," began Zac, looking round at the expectant faces of his audience, "Singing songs of faith, while onlookers are watching and listening reminds me of this story.

"The walls of the dungeon were wet and slimy, and the smell in the inner chamber was revolting. Right in the middle, the two newest prisoners were chained in the stocks, their ankles rubbing uncomfortably on the rough timbers, and their backs bleeding from the professional beating they had just endured from the Roman soldiers. It was midnight and they had no idea what the next day would bring. Would they be beaten again? Would they be executed? They didn't know, but they would never have been able to guess what was to happen in the darkest hour of the night.

"The two men were friends, and followers of Jesus, and in the middle of this awful situation, instead of moaning and complaining, the other prisoners were amazed to hear Paul and Silas begin to sing."[5]

Zac went on to tell of their incredible escape, and everyone was enthralled by his version of the jailer who came to faith.

The next morning was Independence Day, and what a fabulous morning it was. In fact the children had a marvellous day altogether, full of so many memories, that would keep them chatting for years about what they had seen and heard.

The sun was shining, and the whole Rendezvous was up bright and early, with everyone getting into their finest costumes.

Pip and Beth were really excited. This was their special day, the reason they had come to America, and to be perfectly honest, they were both feeling a little nervous. Beth had butterflies in her stomach.

Nanna and Gramps seemed to know exactly how they felt, and gave them lots of advice about what to wear, and what to do. Zac didn't do biscuits and gravy that day, but brought in two plates full of egg sandwiches and a pile of hot buttered muffins. Beth, who thought she wasn't going to be able to eat anything at all, found the muffins just right, and Pip always liked an egg butty.

Soon they were all ready. Although the sun was brightly shining, because it was still quite early, it was a little cool, and the children were glad of their beautiful suede jackets, with the leather tassels and bead decorations. It did make them think about Grey Wolf, and the incident in the museum last night, but they decided not to mention it to anyone else, just yet. Everyone was so busy.

The parade that morning was amazing. There were lots of people involved, most of them in fancy dress. Lots of them were in tribal costumes, or dressed in historical outfits, but there were also people there as fairytale characters, and TV personalities. The police officers were on horseback, dressed in brown and yellow uniforms. At first Pip thought they were in costume, too, but Zac explained that they normally looked like that. The mounted police started the procession, with Pip, Beth and Zac immediately behind them, leading the way through the town.

Pip had been watching when Zac had shown Gramps how to use the black powder guns on the Rendezvous. The black gunpowder is measured and then gently poured into the muzzle of the gun, then the lead ball, which was about the size of a large ball bearing is dropped on top. Next a small piece of cloth is rammed down the muzzle with a thin metal rod, to keep it all in place. As the hammer is pulled back, a small brass cap is fitted over the firing pin, so that when the trigger is released it hits the brass cap. This holds just a small amount of gunpowder. The impact causes it to explode, setting off the main charge, which then fires the ball and cloth together from the barrel of the gun. Pip noticed that there was a strong click, as the firing pin was cocked. Finally, when you pulled the trigger, there was a loud bang, as the charge exploded and sent the small metal ball flying through the air.

Today almost all the adults from the Rendezvous were using the guns in the street, which seemed almost unbelievable. The only difference was that today, instead of firing a metal ball, the guns were being loaded with rolled up silver foil, which streamed out in bright shiny tails when they were fired. Pip noticed that they were still making as much noise as if they were shooting the proper ammunition. It would never happen in England. Pip loved it!

There was so much noise; there were the guns, and all the Indians playing their drums, and then there were marching bands and cheerleaders. The children were in the front of the procession, leading the way around the town, until they arrived back at the museum grounds where a long table had been prepared for lunch.

Beth found it quite overwhelming. By the time they had eaten the celebration lunch, with more bands playing and drums pounding, followed by the speeches by all the town officials and all the clapping and cheering, she was beginning to feel quite dizzy. She was glad that she and Pip were not expected to do anything until later in the afternoon, when they were to hand out the prizes.

She had a real headache coming on and was quite relieved when Nanna suggested that she should have a lie down in the tipi. By now the day had become very hot, and she was surprised at how cool it was under the canvas, with the smoke flaps wide open, and a breeze gently blowing through. The competitions were quite a way away from the encampment, so it was remarkably quiet, too.

Nanna tucked her under a single cotton sheet, and promised that she would look in on her, in an hour or so, to see if she was up to helping at the presentation ceremony. Beth didn't think that she would be able to sleep, but she was wrong. She snuggled down, and was in fact soon fast asleep.

While Beth was resting, Pip had been watching the tomahawk competition. He saw that Zac had been right about how accurate the locals were. Lots of people had had a go at the beginning; even he and Gramps had a throw.

It was a knock out tournament. They had to throw the 'hawks' at a target painted onto a slice of tree trunk. The hawks whistled as they flew through the air, embedding themselves several inches into the wood. The first time Pip tried, the tomahawk just bounced off the target, to lie on the ground. He realized he would have to throw much harder, if he was to succeed.

It was fun to have a go, but when the contest began in earnest, he and Gramps were content to watch the skill of the other competitors. The afternoon wore on, until finally only half a dozen Natives were left. The atmosphere became rather charged with excitement, with different groups shouting for their champions.

Pip and Gramps were facing the targets, so that they could get the best view, but after about half an hour, Pip had the odd feeling that he was being watched. He turned just in time to see a familiar grey-clad figure move from the back of the crowd to the throwing line. Pip had forgotten all about him, and was really surprised to see that Grey Wolf had turned up so late in the event.

9

Whispers

Beth awoke sometime later to the sound of murmured voices, just outside their tipi. Her headache had gone and at first she thought it was someone coming to wake her. She glanced at her watch and she realised that she had only been asleep for about twenty minutes. Nanna wasn't due back for quite a while. She turned over to try to go back to sleep, but the voices became a little louder, and she found herself listening to an odd conversation, or more precisely, one half of a conversation.

"You've got some nice gear on your stall," whispered the first voice, "But just take a look at this."

Beth couldn't really hear the reply; the voice was so low.

"I know it's only a black and white picture," the whisperer continued. "But look at the size of the rubies, and all that gold."

The muttered reply went on longer than before, but Beth still could not make out what was said.

"I'm watching their every move. I'm not going to let them get it. I intend to get away with this necklace before anyone can stop me. You see if I don't!"

This time Beth thought the answer sounded more like a growl, than anything else.

"Look, I've tracked it all this way, I'm sure it's here somewhere, hidden nearby—it's got to be!"

There was a pause, "Now, I'm after a deal," went on the whispering voice, "If I can get my hands on it before they do, would you be able to sell it on for me? I'd split some of the takings with you."

By now the voices had begun to trail off, and Beth guessed that the speakers were moving further away from the tipi. She soon fell asleep again, and dreamt about a fabulous crimson necklace, which she had to wear for the Presentation Ceremony. When she woke a little later she wondered whether it had all been a dream, or whether there really was another treasure to be found. She was actually feeling much better when Nanna did come to take her back to the celebrations.

Pip and Gramps were watching the end of the tomahawk competition. As Grey Wolf walked forward to take his place ready to throw in the contest, Zac announced him, through the speaker system.

"Now that we are into the final round," he said, "Let's welcome last year's champion!"

There was quite a round of applause, and then everyone settled down to watch the finale. It was down to Grey Wolf and another Indian from the Sioux Tribe, who had lots of supporters shouting for him, each time he threw the axe. Gradually the targets were moved further and further back, to test the skill of the marksmen. At first when Grey Wolf took the stand there was total silence, but each time his proved to be the more accurate throw, and in the end everyone was enthusiastically applauding his skill.

By the time Nanna and Beth came to join them, everything was ready for the Presentation Ceremony. Zac was standing at the back of a large table filled with cups and plaques to be awarded, and he was holding a long list of names. Firstly he introduced the children as the 'Honoured Guests' and explained about the twinning of the two towns. Then he asked them a few questions about the mystery that they had solved last year, and finally asked them if they would present the prizes today.

They smiled and said they would. As he called out each of the winners, the person would come forward, and either Pip or Beth would give them the trophy that Zac indicated, and shake their hand. There was a lot of cheering and applause, smiles and hugs of congratulation. Beth was feeling much better, and thoroughly enjoyed herself.

She hadn't had time to chat to Pip before the presentation began, so she was as surprised as he had been to see Grey Wolf among the winners. They both had the strangest feeling when he came up at the end to receive his award; he just gave them both the smallest hint of a smile, as he shook their hands and took his prize, a brass plaque, engraved with the picture of a tomahawk.

"What was all that about?" Beth wondered with a shudder. Pip just shrugged, but generally the children had really enjoyed being a special part of a very special day.

But the day was not over yet. There was a huge barbeque and hog roast, next. Great big steaks, and whole chickens were barbequed, and a large pit had been dug at the side of the presentation table. It was a much deeper pit than the one outside their tipi. It needed to be, because throughout the day a whole pig had been gently roasting, filling the air with a lovely smell. Beth found that she was really hungry, now, and enjoyed sitting at the head of the table, tucking into a huge sandwich, filled with the softest, tastiest, shredded roast pork.

The evening concluded with the traditional firework display on the riverside. It was awesome, with bigger fireworks than the children had ever seen. They had brought chairs and rugs from the Rendezvous, and were sitting in groups, along the riverbank, drinking hot fruit punch and nibbling on chunks of homemade fudge.

A huge red and yellow firework soared overhead, trailing sparkling tails in all directions. Pip watched one of these tails whizzing overhead, and then turned to watch it cascade into the blackness behind him, in the direction of the encampment.

The Rendezvous site was in darkness, as everyone had come over to the riverside, to enjoy the spectacular display. As the firework went out, Pip noticed, just in the corner of his eye, a triangle of light amid the tents and tipis. He turned to look properly, and realised that someone was obviously inside one of the tipis.

He remembered Dancing Spring telling them that people outside would see their silhouette if they used a light inside their tent. Pip found himself able to watch a figure moving around, bending and straightening, going all round the edges of the tipi. He thought the person must have lost something. The light of a torch was easily visible moving around inside the tipi. Suddenly the torchlight shone upwards, illuminated another silhouette, high up on the side of the tipi. There was some kind of design, near the smoke-flaps.

'It looks a bit like the rays of the sun that is on our tipi,' thought Pip, and then he remembered that theirs was the only decorated tipi on site, all the others were plain white. He peered into the now darkened campsite; the torch had been switched off, and there was no one to be seen.

'Could someone have been inside their tent?' he wondered. Perhaps Nanna had sent Gramps to get her another blanket; she was always pretty cold outside, late at night.

Suddenly a large, bright firework exploded high above them, and Beth reached over and grabbed his arm, pointing to the many coloured fountains streaming through the night sky.

"You're missing all the fun!" she said, and he had to admit that the rest of the display was so stunning that he forgot all about the shadow in the tipi, until much later that night, when something rather sinister reminded him of what he had seen.

It was almost midnight when the last good-bye had been said, and everything had been packed up, all the rugs and chairs, cups, flasks and lanterns ready to be carried back to the tipi. They were all quite quiet, reliving memories of the fun, as they crossed the open grassy area.

"Well, what a fantastic day," Gramps eventually murmured, lifting the tipi's canvas door, so that Nanna could climb in.

The entrance to the tipi was a hole, about two foot above the ground, which was covered by the canvas door flap with the picture of the buffalo skull painted on it. Pip was holding a lantern, so that Nanna didn't trip as she strode over the entrance.

Once Nanna was inside, Pip passed the lantern in to her.

"Oh, no!" she immediately exclaimed.

Pip pushed his head through the opening.

"How awful!" he said as soon as he saw what she was looking at.

Gramps ducked his head through the door, too. "What is it?" he asked, but saw straight away that their tipi was in a real mess. There were blankets everywhere, the ones that should have been on the beds were strewn around on the floor, while the ones they had used as rugs had all been pulled up, and left in heaps. All their cases had been emptied and the contents scattered amongst the blankets. By now all four of them were inside the tent, looking at the damage.

"Well, I never!" exclaimed Nanna, shaking her head.

"I can't believe it," said Gramps. "I don't imagine you left it like this when you came to get Beth."

"We certainly didn't!" answered Nanna.

"I know that Zac told us that during the day visitors were allowed to wander around the Rendezvous and look inside the tents," said Beth, "But surely they wouldn't make a mess like this."

"I'm sure they wouldn't," said Gramps. "This looks like someone has been searching for valuables. What a good thing we left all our passports and stuff in the safe in the museum."

"Gramps?" said Pip, suddenly remembering the shadows he had seen during the firework display. "I think I might have seen them."

"What do you mean?" asked Gramps.

Pip explained.

"Why on earth didn't you tell us?" asked Gramps.

"I know the fireworks were exciting," put in Nanna, "But why didn't you say something?"

Pip wished he had done, but there was nothing he could do about it now. And that was exactly what Gramps said.

"Well, there's nothing we can do about it now. It's been a long day, and we are all tired. Just have a quick check to see if anything is missing, but there was nothing in here of any value, so I won't bother the others with the news until the morning. You two get some sleep. I don't suppose ours has been the only tent to be searched. I hope no one has lost anything worth a lot of money."

Beth had waited until there was silence from their grandparents' side of the tent. Pip was almost asleep, too, but the moment she urgently whispered his name, he was wide-awake again. She told him all about the conversation she had overheard that afternoon. He was intrigued.

"So they were talking about a necklace?" he asked. "I wonder . . ." he mused.

"I thought it might be something to do with our mystery," said Beth.

"I was thinking the same. Who do you think it was?" he asked.

"I'm not sure," she answered, "I could only really hear one side of the conversation. The other person just seemed to grunt." Even as she said the word 'grunt', a picture of the grey-clad Indian slipped into her mind. "Perhaps it was . . ." she began, but Pip interrupted her.

"Grey Wolf!" he whispered excitedly. They were both remembering the way the Indian hardly seemed to say anything at all when they first met him; in fact most of his answers could have been described as grunts.

"It could have been," Beth answered, thoughtfully.

"So he and somebody else are searching for a ruby necklace," pondered Pip. "I wonder if that was who was searching in here?"

"We'll have to have a proper look around tomorrow, in the light," she suggested.

"A ruby necklace," repeated Pip, slowly. "I wonder if that really was what Rose wanted Isaac to find? I wonder if that's why she left all those clues."

"Real treasure, this time," said Beth, dreamily. "Wouldn't that be good?" she asked.

"Mmm," came the sleepy reply, and soon both children were fast asleep, dreaming of rubies and gold.

10

The Fort

Quite early the following morning they woke to hear Gramps leaving the tipi.

"I'm just going to tell Zac and Timothy about the problem last night," he said, then, "Oh, hello, Peter! Come to take them off to the fort?"

The children had forgotten that they had arranged to go, but it only took a moment for them to put on their ordinary clothes, swallow a quick OJ, as the Americans called orange juice, and pick up their things and go.

Peter had come to take them to visit Fort Clatsop, the place where Lewis and Clark had spent the winter with their Indian guide, Sacagawea, in 1805. They piled all their things into his camper van, and Pip jumped into the front seat, leaving Beth to ride in the back. She didn't mind, and enjoyed watching the forest slip by, as Peter and Pip chatted in the front.

The Fort proved to be much smaller than they had expected, especially as it had apparently housed over fifty people. There were guides here in costumes similar to the ones people were wearing on the Rendezvous. They were telling the visitors all about life in the Fort, which was called 'Clatsop' in honour of the local Indian Tribe. Lewis and Clark were explorers, and were the first white people to cross the continent. They had arrived at the mouth of the Columbia River in 1805, as winter set in. They had built this place to shelter them, as they hunted the local forests and gathered what food they could in the area around, processing salt out of the seawater from the near-by beach, to use on their return journey.

At first the children enjoyed listening, but Pip soon got a little bored, and was really pleased when Peter suggested they went down to the riverside to watch a Native American building a canoe. Beth was really interested in the fort, so they said that they would come and find her when the canoe was finished. Peter told them that there was the chance that they might be able to ride downstream in the dugout, once it was finished, and try it out.

The guys had gone, and Beth was enjoying listening to their guide skilfully weaving stories of adventure with true facts about the history of the fort. The guide was a young Indian girl only a few years older than Pip. She was dressed in a beautiful deerskin tunic, her long hair braided into two plaits, fastened with bright turquoise beads. She showed them pictures of the fifteen-year-old Sacagawea, a young princess of the Shoshone tribe, who had helped the explorers cross the Indian country.

Fleet Foot, as the guide was called, took them into the small room that had been made to look exactly like the one Lewis and Clark would have shared. The whole fort had been made from the trees of the nearby forest. In here the beds, chairs and table were also made of new, pale gold timbers.

Fleet Foot explained that the explorers had brought everything else over the difficult mountain trails with them. At first they had travelled as part of a wagon train, later their things would have been transferred to the backs of ponies and donkeys, and finally, over the most difficult paths, they would have had to carry things by hand. Although the journey had been very difficult, Beth thought it all sounded exciting and romantic. She could imagine the thrill of discovering new lands.

"And this is where the journey ended, in a very wet season. That whole winter long," Fleet Foot explained, "They only had eleven days when it didn't rain. They were cooped up in their tiny, little rooms for weeks on end."

Beth shuddered; it seemed a cold and sad end to their journey.

"At least Lewis and Clark had plenty to do," Fleet Foot added. "Clark was the cartographer," she explained. "It was his job to draw the maps, so that others would be able to follow their journey in the future, and open up this whole area to pioneers. Lewis was the artist."

She pointed out a large, dark wooden box at the foot of Lewis' bed.

"This is the very sea chest that Lewis carried all the way from the East," she said. She opened it, and pointed out that it contained his journals and notebooks full of his drawings. "He recorded all the animals and plants that they had seen, as well as writing about the different tribes they encountered." She showed them a faded yellow paper with a Native American dressed in what Beth recognised as 'full regalia', his complete ceremonial outfit.

As the other visitors began to leave the room Beth had a better chance to look around. She wanted to see Lewis' drawing books. She knew that they were only replicas of his original sketches, but recently she had been studying wild flowers, and Fleet Foot had said that he had drawn the many new species of plants they had discovered. At last she managed to get close enough to the sea chest to see. But what really caught her eye was not the drawing book, but the chest itself. It looked exactly like the one they had brought into their tipi, with the blankets in, the one from Rose's bedroom.

"Oh," she said, "This is just like the box we have been using on the Rendezvous!"

"Really?" asked Fleet Foot, who had stayed in the room, too.

"We call it a blanket box, but what did you say it was?" asked Beth.

"It's a sea chest," answered the guide. "People would fill these, not just with blankets," she explained, "But with all their most treasured possessions. Look!"

She opened the chest, and showed Beth how it contained a special locked compartment, right at the bottom. "For all your valuable documents," she added, and with a flourish she drew out of her jacket pocket a silver key. Then she bent down to unlock the now empty section of the sea chest.

"Wow!" exclaimed Beth, slipping her hand into her own pocket, where she kept the key from the drawer in the clock. She didn't take it out, but she could hardly wait to tell Pip what she had just found out. Perhaps there was a special compartment in Rose's chest in their tipi.

Peter and Pip came to collect Beth soon after that. They had enjoyed watching the making of the canoe, and now they had the chance to be the first to try it out. There was room for just two of them with the Indian builder, and Peter had suggested that the children go.

The trip down the river in the canoe was so much fun. They were equipped with bright orange life jackets and a paddle each. Their guide showed them how to use long smooth strokes in the deep, slowly flowing river. They paddled downstream about half a mile, and then the river narrowed and they could hear the sound of the water rushing over some large stones up ahead. Their guide indicated that they should paddle over to the bank, before they got to the rapids. They helped him to manoeuvre their boat into the bank.

The Fort's own jeep was parked at the riverside. Standing beside it were some adult guests, who had canoed before. They were going to try the little craft over the rapids. Pip and Beth clambered out of the canoe, using their oars to steady them, and then handing them over to the other people. They stood for a few moments, watching the little boat until it turned the corner, out of sight. Then the children got into the jeep, to return to the Fort.

It was not until they were driving back in the jeep that Beth at last had her opportunity to tell Pip her news about the sea chest.

"The blanket box from Rose's room," she began, "Is exactly the same as the sea chest in the fort," she whispered, excitedly. "The guide at the fort had told me that most people would pack all their belongings into a chest like that, when they were going on a long sea voyage."

Pip looked a little puzzled.

"Rose came all the way from England, right across the Atlantic," she continued. "Fleet Foot also said that many people who intended to cross the continent from East to West, like Lewis and Clark had done, would be often take a sea chest like that on the wagon-train."

"Rose would have had to do the same journey," Pip said, realising what this meant. "She had to cross from the East to the West coast."

"That's right," added Beth, "She could have continued to use her 'chest' all the way here. And best of all," she added, quickly, just as they drew up in the car park at the fort, "The key Fleet Foot had was almost the same as the key from the clock!"

Pip could only stare at her in amazement, but she put her fingers to her lips, as Peter walked over to meet them. Pip nodded his agreement; they both thought that it would be best not to mention it to anyone else, just yet.

When they got back to the fort they were just in time to watch the enactment of the arrival of the explorers, before it was time to return to the Rendezvous. Somehow the journey back seemed to take much longer than the trip there that morning. It was Beth's turn to ride in the front, but after driving for about half an hour Pip noticed that she was beginning to doze. Peter was also quiet at the wheel, so Pip, who was not usually interested in the scenery, found himself with nothing to do but gaze out of the window.

They had been travelling through some of the vast forests almost since leaving the modern village of Clatsop, close to the fort. The hills, which had been quite steep, were now levelling out, and it was as the trees were beginning to thin out that he thought he saw a figure standing just inside the tree line. As they drew alongside Pip was sure he could make out the figure of Grey Wolf standing still in the half-light, his wolf beside him, its nose raised, sniffing the air. Could he have been there just waiting for them? Just what was going on?

When eventually they arrived at the Rendezvous Peter parked his van by his tent, and the children went back to their tipi.

"Don't forget to put yer Indian clothes back on!" called Peter as they ran off.

"We won't!" shouted Pip.

"And thanks for a great day!" added Beth.

They could hardly wait to get back to the tipi and have a proper look inside the sea chest. It was with great excitement that they hurried in. Nanna and Gramps had gone over with Timothy to the tipi of some of his friends. The whole family and honoured guests had been invited to eat with them later that evening. Pip and Beth knew where to find that tipi, over the other side of the field. Now they were glad that they had their own tipi to themselves.

Nanna had tidied up all the mess from the night before. She had used most of the blankets from the chest, and it didn't take Pip long to pull the final few out of the bottom. They had never noticed before, but now they could easily see the small, special compartment on the left hand side at the bottom. It was exactly like the special document compartment that Fleet Foot had shown Beth in Lewis' sea chest.

But immediately the children were disappointed. They could see that although the compartment had been lockable, it wasn't locked any more. It was obvious that the lock had been smashed. At first Pip thought that it must have happened a long time ago, but as he bent down for a closer look he could see that the splinters of wood were fresh and clean.

"Oh, no!" he said, groaning.

Beth moved round so that she could look inside easier.

"It looks as though that's only been done recently," said Pip.

"Oh, no!" Beth echoed.

"Wait a minute," he said; "You don't think it might have happened yesterday when I saw a silhouette of someone moving furtively around in here? I thought that it might have been Gramps, looking for another blanket for Nanna but obviously it wasn't. Do you think that whoever was searching in here must have found that compartment?"

"That would mean that if there was anything to find, it will be gone now," said Beth, remembering what he had told her last night. "This was probably our only good lead," she added, the disappointment evident in her voice.

"I know," muttered Pip.

Even though the lock had been forced, Pip felt that he ought to at least try to see if the key from the clock fitted. Beth already had it out of her pocket; she passed it over and he bent to slide it into the lock. It fitted perfectly, and he found that when he turned it the metal part moved into place, even though the slot that it should have gone into had been smashed and broken.

"Well, it's even more disappointing to know that this really was the right chest," he said, glumly. "Whatever was hidden in there has been taken, now."

"We'd better tidy up," said Beth, going to collect the blankets and put them back inside the chest. Gramps had placed the chest right in the middle of the tipi, at the point where the makeshift walls met. To replace the blankets Beth had to move the curtain dividing the two areas of the tent. Sunlight was streaming through the top of the tipi now, and one golden beam shone straight into the bottom of the chest.

"Just a minute," she said, letting the blankets fall to the floor, "Look at this!" She pointed into the corner of the lockable compartment. The sunlight seemed to pick out a strange mark, right in the angle where the two planks met. Pip could see something scratched in the bottom corner, on the floor of the compartment.

He peered closer to see something like a zigzag mark.

"Oh, yes!" he said, "I see what you mean."

"It looks like a letter Z," said Beth.

"Z?" asked Pip.

"Yes, like in the Mark of Zorro, the sign that he carved in the wall, and things."

"Oh, yeah, I get it," said Pip. "Z for . . ."

"How about Z for Zac; you know, she used to call Isaac Zac, didn't she?" Beth suggested.

"It could be!" he agreed and he knelt down to examine the mark a little closer. He ran his finger along the bottom, which was rough from the fragments of wood that had fallen down when the lock had been forced.

"Ouch," he cried, as one of the splinters stabbed into his finger. He pushed his finger down hard to try to make the pain go away, then as he pulled his hand up, to put the painful finger straight into his mouth both children heard a soft click, and the base panel of the document compartment gently slid aside to reveal another secret compartment.

"Wow!" they said in unison.

11

A Secret Place

There at the bottom of the box was a small, secret compartment. Pip bent down and slid his hand inside. He drew out what he thought was a small, thin book. It was made of tooled leather, with a simple design of leaves on the front.

All pain forgotten for the moment, both children sat together on Beth's bed as Pip undid the leather straps that fastened the leather bound outer covers. When he did they could see that this wasn't a book, but a writing case. On the left-hand side were a number of unused faded envelopes, and on the right-hand side, yellowed sheets of paper, with writing on the top one.

The other sheets were empty, but tucked behind them there was a small, pale green, fairly thick piece of card.

"It looks like a bus ticket," said Beth. It was a ticket, not for a bus, but for an ocean-going liner. It was a single ticket, and they could just make out the names 'Liverpool' and 'New York', in faded ink. As Pip was pulling this out a tiny piece of paper fluttered to the floor. It had been cut out of a newspaper, and was covered on both sides with tiny print. They peered closely, but the lettering was difficult to see, so they replaced both it and the ticket in the back of the case, and turned again to the top sheet of writing paper.

The upper half of this sheet had some names, written in fancy writing. The first was Rosemary Davis, then John Howarth and Rosemary Howarth, and three names: Rosy Davis, Rosie Davison and finally Rose Davidson. The last three names had been copied out a number of times, in different styles.

"Look!" Pip pointed out, "All the R's are exactly the same." They were. Each had a smooth, round semicircle at the top, that started a good way to the left of the downward-stroke, and then they all finished with the right-hand leg of the R twisting under all the other letters, and then curling into a little flourish.

"So they are," agreed Beth. "Almost as if she had been practising," she mused.

They looked at the bottom half of the page. This contained a very fancy family crest. The lettering was so fancy that if he hadn't just been reading the names earlier on the page, Pip thought he wouldn't have been able to work out the word Howarth, at the centre of the shield.

"Well, that's not much of a find!" said Pip. "It was hardly worth stabbing my finger."

"I bet that hurt," sympathised Beth, who had forgotten the splinter. "Let's have a look!"

Pip held his finger out towards her, and although she could see the piece of wood she could tell that it would not be easy to pull out again simply with her fingers.

"I think that we are going to need one of Nanna's needles," she said, going into their grandparents' section of the tipi. Nanna always kept a spare needle in her reading-glasses' case. It was threaded with black cotton, but Beth didn't think that would make any difference to the job in hand. They both knew that it was always better to remove a splinter as quickly as possible.

She had been doing her first aid course at Guides that year, so soon she was burrowing away with a needle, trying to get the splinter out. Pip actually preferred to watch what she was doing, even though he was sweating like mad. Finally she managed to make a small opening in the skin, exposing the sliver of wood, but to get it out she had to slide the point of the needle underneath, which hurt so much that Pip pulled his finger away. In doing so he knocked the needle out of her hand, and saw that he had drawn blood. He had moved the splinter though, so at least he had the satisfaction of getting it out himself. He sucked it clean, once the grains of wood were out.

Beth was looking for the dropped needle. It had landed inside the blanket box, or sea chest, as they now knew that it was called. If she had taken the thread off it, she probably would not have seen it so easily, however she could make out the black cotton trailing over the edge of the compartment, and into the secret panel. As she leaned in to get it out, it dropped further in. She had to reach right into the secret hole, and still the needle was awkward to get out. It seemed to be stuck on something. She tugged, and the needle did move towards her, bringing with it part of some dark blue velvet material.

"What's this?" she asked, taking hold of the velvet and pulling it out of its hidden corner, into the light. It was a small, blue bag, with a drawstring top. By now Pip was at her side.

"Open it!" he demanded, unnecessarily, because Beth was already tipping the heavy contents out.

Some large, red rubies fell onto Beth's hand, followed by strings of smaller ones, and some pieces of twisted gold. The sunlight was still streaming through the roof, so the children could see straight away that they had found something very special.

"At last," said Pip, voicing what they were both thinking, "Real treasure!"

They carefully spread out the jewels on Beth's bed. The Indian blanket she had chosen for the top of hers had deep furrows in and some of the smaller pieces sank into it.

"Just a minute," said Pip, and went to get a clean white tee-shirt from his case. "It'll show up better on this."

When they had taken care to move all the little pieces of the necklace, as well as the long strings of rubies onto the white material they were able to see much better. There were three strands of beautiful rubies threaded among little links of gold. Next there were four much larger rubies, two of which had heavy, intricate gold surrounds fixed to them; the other two had the remains of their settings, chunky bits of gold, which looked as if they had been broken, and the bigger parts of the gold were missing. Then there were a couple of dozen loose, small rubies, some with the remains of their chain still attached and bits of rough, twisted pieces of gold. Finally there was one huge crimson ruby, completely without any of its setting, but which seemed to trap the sunlight deep in its heart when Beth lifted it up to the light, cupped in her hand. It almost covered her palm.

She gasped with delight.

This was real treasure. This had to be the ruby necklace the whisperers had been talking about. Suddenly a shiver ran down her neck as she remembered the guy with the picture. 'I'm watching their every move,' he had said. 'I'll get it whatever it takes.' Beth quickly looked around the tipi, but of course it was empty.

"Pip," she found herself whispering, "If this is what the whisperer was after, he said that he was not going to let anyone stop him getting the necklace. What will he do when he finds out that we have it?"

"Then we'd better take it to safety, right now!" said Pip.

The children realised that they must take their find straight to the adults. It was nearly suppertime, and they knew that everyone had been invited over to Timothy's friends' cooking pit for their meal. Beth carefully scooped up all the jewels and Pip held the velvet bag open for them, then securely fastened the draw string and put the bag deep into his pocket. Beth closed the writing case and tied its leather strings back together again, so that nothing could fall out. She slipped it inside her drawing bag, and they set off.

They were surprised at how late it was getting, when they opened the tipi door. What an eventful day they had had, and what news they had to tell. They intended to go straight to Timothy's friends' tipi, however their plans were changed almost as soon as they were outside. Normally when they left their tipi they simply had to cross a large empty grassy area in the middle of the Rendezvous. Pip was a little annoyed, because today it seemed as though everyone on the encampment was standing around in a huge circle, which meant that they couldn't easily get across the field.

He began to go around the back of the group, peering through the onlookers to see what they were watching. He could hear the pow-wow drums beating out a strong rhythm, but he couldn't see because of all the people.

Beth had stopped, too, obviously interested in what was going on. "It reminds me of Rose's favourite story," she said.

"What?" asked Pip.

"You know! Zacchaeus! Climbing a tree to see what the crowd was looking at," she answered.

"Oh, yes," said Pip. "Well, there are no trees near enough, but we could push through the people if you want to."

By now both children were keen to see what was going on, besides, the jewels were safely in Pip's pocket, so what was the harm in stopping for a minute or two?

It didn't take them long to ease their way through the crowd of grown-ups, until they were in the front row. They found that they were watching an exciting display of Native Dancing. There were a number of people playing the drums, but right in the middle of the open space an Indian brave in 'full regalia', his complete Native costume, was leaping and dancing, twisting and turning dramatically in time with the beat.

It really was quite exciting to watch. He was dressed in long tan trousers, with lots of leather tassels on them. His chest was mostly bare, and he was wearing a long breastplate of bone, metal and leather around his neck. On his head was a huge plumed headdress of black and white eagles feathers. His face was painted in strong stripes of red and black war paint, and looked quite terrifying.

He was holding a tomahawk in one hand, and a war lance in his other hand. This was an elaborate stick, with a knife blade at the top. It was decorated with eagle feathers and long tassels of leather, some tan and some dark red, more than a foot long. The effect was very dramatic as the drum beat increased in speed. Finally he spun around and came to a halt with the last beat of the drum, lowering his head to the floor, while the audience cheered in delight.

The children were just about to move away and seek out their grandparents, when the Indian suddenly straightened up, gazing right into Pip's face, his piecing gray eyes holding the boy's for a moment or two. A shiver went down Pip's spine. Behind the brightly coloured war paint Pip had not recognized the Indian, but he would have known those eyes anywhere. The dancer was Grey Wolf!

12

To the Rescue!

For a second Pip froze. Then his fingers closed instinctively around the jewel pouch in his pocket. Without thinking, he grabbed Beth's hand, turning to shout to her over the noise of the applause.

"Run!" he called.

Beth had recognized Grey Wolf too, so she didn't need any more persuading. They went rushing back through the crowd, then around the outside of the circle, arriving at the other side of the field, close to the tipi they were seeking, a few minutes later. Timothy's friends had chosen to pitch their tent under some alder trees, which gave shade during the hot summer days, but at this time in the evening it did make their site a little dark.

As soon as they were within earshot, Pip began calling out, "Gramps, Nanna! Come and look at this!"

The children passed the first couple of trees at the side of the white tipi and found everyone in the front of tent, from where they had been able to watch the show.

"Gramps, Nanna!" called Pip, out of breath from running.

Everyone immediately looked over at the children, who were by now quite hot and bothered. Gramps and Zac stood at the side of the fire pit, where Timothy and his friend were straightening up from the cooking, to see what the shouting was about. Nanna and Bella May were sitting on folding chairs, looking expectantly over at the children.

"Look what we've found!" called Pip, striding over, full of excitement.

"What?" asked Gramps and Zac, in unison.

Pip had come to a standstill under a tall tree, facing Gramps and Zac, and now he drew the velvet pouch out of his pocket. He was looking down at that, and trying to open the cord, so it was only Beth, who was standing next to him who saw the look of horror pass over Gramps' face. Gramps wasn't looking at his grandson anymore, but at something behind both Pip and herself.

Beth twisted round to see, and at that moment Pip heard a familiar click. He had been hearing it most of the time on the Rendezvous, especially during the parade, but tonight, out here in the deepening evening shadows, the sound seemed louder and more sinister. He knew what it was. It was the hammer of a black powder gun being cocked, and it seemed to be coming from somewhere just behind him. He froze.

"I'll take that!" ordered a voice behind him. "Hand it over, now!"

Pip, half expecting to see Grey Wolf, turned to face the speaker, but instead was truly amazed to see Peter. He was leaning back against a tree, in an almost casual pose. One hand was outstretched towards Pip, but there was nothing casual about the way he was holding the loaded pistol in his other hand. It was a smaller version of the muskets they had been carrying before, and just as deadly.

"Now, just a minute," began Zac.

"I mean it!" demanded Peter, deliberately aiming the gun straight at Pip. "I'm not afraid to use this. I've come so far. It's taken me months. Those jewels belong to me," he said, looking first at Zac, and then at Gramps. "Step away, you two!" he ordered.

They had no option but to do so.

"And now!" he said to Pip, "Give that to me!"

He leaned forward as he spoke, and as he did so he snapped a twig beneath his feet. The sound seemed so loud in the tension of the moment that Beth's eyes were drawn down to his moccasin covered feet. She gasped. She would know those moccasins anywhere. They were the ones she had seen while she was hiding under the ball dress. They didn't belong to Grey Wolf at all.

Pip and Beth could hardly believe what was happening. So it was Peter all along. As they tried to come to terms with this new revelation, Pip stared into Peter's eyes and saw the look of grim determination on his face. It was the look of a man who really did mean what he said.

The friendly mask had been dropped and the real Peter stood before them.

Pip knew he had no choice, even without seeing the look of horror on his grandfather's face. Very reluctantly he took a step forward and held the blue bag out towards Peter.

"They're mine!" crowed Peter in delight, but the words were hardly out of his mouth when a sudden movement caught Pip's eye. Peter's fingers were just closing around the jewel pouch when there was another familiar sound.

Whiz! Thump!

All eyes turned in astonishment to see a tomahawk had buried itself in the tree behind Peter, pinning his jacket firmly to the trunk by the sleeve, narrowly missing his arm.

Peter dropped the gun. It clattered to the floor, and he almost lost his grip on the bag of rubies. But immediately he shrugged, pulled his arm out of his coat and ran off into the forest, leaving his jacket pinned to the tree.

A piercing whistle rang out through the trees, and the baying of a wolf shattered the evening air. Pip didn't have to look behind him to see who had thrown the tomahawk; he had guessed it was Grey Wolf, even before his young wolf pushed past him, chasing after Peter.

Pip almost felt as if he was dreaming. He saw Peter running at full speed through the forest, towards the clearing, where his van was parked. Hard on his heels followed the grey shape of the wolf, his lips in an angry snarl and a deep guttural sound coming from his throat. A scream split the air as the wolf leaped on its prey, his front paws planted firmly on Peter's shoulders.

"Stay!" came the shout of command, as Grey Wolf, still wearing his awesome native 'regalia', strode majestically after them, into the clearing.

Gramps and the children came quickly through the woods, to find Peter pinned to the ground by Grey Wolf's magnificent animal.

"Get this thing off me!" Peter wailed.

Zac wasn't far behind them. "You'll stay there!" he demanded. "Timothy is calling the police and they'll be here in a few minutes. Meanwhile I'll take those!" he said, bending over Peter's fallen body, and taking the blue pouch out of his grip. "Whatever they are, they don't belong to you."

13

Another Find

The rest of the night was taken up with interviews with the police. Peter had been taken away. A kind faced detective, who reminded them of their friend Mac, back in England, took a statement outlining all the events. He took details of how they had been followed into the museum, the searching of their tipi and the finding of the jewels.

Taking the largest ruby between his thumb and first finger and lifting it up to the light the detective said, "They'll need valuing properly of course, but I'm pretty sure they're worth a small fortune."

The police agreed to leave the rubies with the museum, but they emphasised that they may be needed later in evidence. Zac and one of the officers went straight to the museum safe and locked them carefully away and then, at long last the police left.

It was to be their last night in the tipi. Once again, everyone gathered around the stove in Timothy and Bella May's tent. It was late in the evening. Their friends had sent them the casserole that they had cooked and it smelled delicious, as they all settled down with bowls and forks and chunks of crusty bread to discuss the day's events. What a story they had to tell.

Beth was so excited that she hardly ate anything, so when they got to the part where they found the jewel bag beneath the writing case, she reached into her drawing bag. Zac had the jewel pouch safely tucked away, but it was the first time the family had had a good chance to look inside the writing case. She now drew it out for everyone to see. The adults all crowded around.

"So you think that this is Rose's writing case?" asked Zac.

Pip and Beth exchanged glances. "Yes!" they said together.

Beth opened it, and first of all lifted out the faded yellow paper with the writing on it.

"Look!" she pointed.

They looked down at the sheet of names.

Rosemary Davis

John and Rosemary Howarth

Rosy Davis

Rosie Davison

Rose Davidson

Before anyone else could say anything Pip began, "All the R's are the same," he said, "As though Rose, Rosie and Rosemary were the same person."

"Oh, yes, I see," said Nanna. "That's a good bit of detective work, Pip."

"We thought," added Beth, "that perhaps Rose had been trying out different signatures."

"What do you mean?" said Bella May, "Do you think that our Rose may not have always had that name. Perhaps she was originally called one of these other names."

"That would explain," said Timothy, "Why all these years we have never been able to find out anything more about Rose Davidson."

"Old Isaac always said that she didn't ever mention her maiden name," added Zac. "Perhaps one of these names is that, but I don't understand why there should be so many variations."

"Was there anything else in the writing case that might give us a clue?" asked Gramps.

Pip passed the small green ticket over to him. "There was this, a ticket from Liverpool to New York, on a liner, and another bit of a newspaper, that we couldn't make out."

"Ah, now then," said Zac, "We knew that she came over from the old country. This might tell us when." He and Gramps peered at it, to see if they could make out a date.

"Right in the top corner," said Gramps, "There seems to be part of a date. It looks like '1st', but the rest of it is missing."

Zac turned the ticket over to examine the back. "I think," he said, pointing, "That says 'April', don't you?"

Gramps squinted at it. "It might do," he admitted, passing the ticket back to Pip, who simply nodded.

"What about the newspaper?" asked Nanna. "There may be a date on that."

Beth passed it over for Nanna to examine, saying, "We couldn't read it, the print was so small, and once we found the rubies, we forgot all about it anyway."

Nanna brought it close to her face, so that she could just about read it. Both sides were covered in print, but she soon realised that one side did not really make sense, on its own, whereas the other side had a short, sad obituary on it, which had been cut out.

"It looks like it is the report of someone's death," she said, squinting down to read it aloud. "This is to report the sudden and tragic death of Young Lord John Haworth, aged 22 years, on Sunday last. He died in a coach accident. Our condolences go to the family. The funeral will be held next week, after the inquest."

"John Howarth!" exclaimed Pip, "That is one of the names on the sheet."

"So it is," said Beth.

"But there is no date," said Nanna.

"So I suppose we will have to leave it for today," said Zac, looking at his watch. "I imagine that you are too tired after all your excitements to want another exciting story to finish the day with." He glanced over at the children with a twinkle in his eye.

"No way!" said Pip, to everyone's surprise, "I'm really enjoying these night time stories. Who would have thought there would be so many tales of adventure in the Bible?"

Everyone laughed and then Zac began.

"Well," started Zac, "I think despite the excitement and thrill of these last few hours, we have all had a nasty shock and a scare." Gramps nodded, and exchanged a look with Nanna.

"You can say that again," she agreed. "We thought we might be going to lose our Pip."

"Exactly," said Gramps.

"It reminded me," said Zac, "Of a time when someone else was in great danger, and from someone who should have been a friend. Let me begin . . .

"After the hubbub and noise began to die down, the music of the harp gently filled the room, and the singer began a beautiful song, encouraging his listeners to trust in God at all times. The fire crackled in the huge grate and the torchlight glinted on the weapons leaning against the wall. The great hall in the palace was full of soldiers, men of all ages and backgrounds who had been telling tales of their adventures, rejoicing in their recent victory."

The children smiled as the story reminded them of the scene around the camp fire the other evening, singing and telling stories.

Zac continued, hinting at the stories they would be telling, battles with the Philistines and the contest with the giant, but just when the story seemed very familiar Zac's voice took on a harsher note: "Suddenly the king, who was standing at the other end of the hall, shouted in rage and the next moment a long spear came hurtling through the air almost pinning young David to the wall." [6]

"Wow!" said Pip, "Just like Grey Wolf's throw, this evening."

"Almost like that!" corrected Zac. "I think if Grey Wolf had meant to kill, Peter would be dead, whereas King Saul did want to kill David, but God protected him."

"Just like God protected Pip, tonight," said Beth, looking over at her brother.

"Exactly!" said Gramps.

"Yes," said Nanna, "We have a lot to be thankful for."

"That's right!" said Zac. "Do you remember one of the songs that David wrote, the one that that tells of the Shepherd's care? There is a verse in that which says 'Even though I walk through the valley of the shadow of death, I will not be afraid, for You are with me.' When I think of that gun pointing at Pip tonight . . ." Zac's voice faltered, he just couldn't go on, and simply shook his head.

Gramps shook his head slowly, too, then he closed his eyes and said, almost in a whisper, but everyone could clearly hear, "Thank You, Lord, for Your protection tonight. Thank You . . . from the bottom of our hearts."

And everyone quietly said, "Amen," and then they gathered up their things and headed off to bed.

News of the arrest had spread and the following day lots of people came to visit the Rendezvous, just to see the scene of all the excitement of the night before. The children must have retold their story dozens of times by the time the last curious visitors had left.

Pip and Beth felt quite sad and tired, by the evening, because it was time to pack up the tipi and head back to Zac's house. They still had a few days of their holiday left, but this was the end of camping-out under the stars at night, cooking on open fires and wearing all the fancy leather and beads. What a holiday it had been!

It was just as they had finished packing up the rest of the Rendezvous, that Timothy decided they should collect all Peter's things, as he was still being held at the police station. He had left his camper van open, in the clearing where he had been arrested, so Timothy went to drive it back to Peter's small one-man tent. He and Gramps then began sorting through things in the van and asked the children to have a look inside the tent.

It felt a little eerie in the half-light, as Pip and Beth bent low to go inside the tent. It was only big enough to sleep one person; it was dark green and only three feet high at the door end, sloping even lower towards the other end. Beth pushed past Pip, going down to the foot end of the tent. Peter had just been sleeping in there, living and cooking in the van, and they didn't expect to find anything other than his sleeping bag and bedroll, but they set about looking for any clues, as to why he had tried to take the jewels.

Beth bent down to take hold of the sleeping bag, and Pip was rather surprised when they began to pull it out, because it felt quite heavy. Beth picked up the foot end, and walked towards him. As she came out of the tent she lifted her end up high, shaking it, until a bundle fell clear of the bag. It was a pair of striped pyjamas, but they had been rolled around something else, something which now slid out of its hiding place to land at Pip's feet.

"It's a rucksack!" she said.

Pip bent down to pick it up. He remembered that Peter had always had the rucksack with him, wherever he went. He pulled open a couple of the straps, to see what was inside, and as he did so a very old exercise book slipped out of the top of it. Nanna, who had been supervising the children, stooped to catch it, and it fell open in her hand.

"Well!" she exclaimed, "I wonder what this is?" The children stood at each side of her, to see. The pages at the beginning of the book had been ruled in pencil, and each line was covered with letters written in a round, childish hand. There were lines of each of the letters of the alphabet, repeated over and over again. Obviously someone had been practicing their handwriting. This went on for many pages.

"It looks like a school-book," said Pip. "How boring!"

"But why bring an old school book on holiday?" asked Nanna, flipping through more pages of writing.

"It changes, here," she noticed, "This time they are copying out verses from the beginning of Genesis. Look!" she added, pointing, "Each verse is repeated many times."

Beth looked. "But the handwriting's not really getting any better, is it?"

Nanna smiled, "You're right there!" she said. "Mind you, it must have been pretty dull," she continued, flicking over the pages. "The entire first chapter of Genesis is here, each new page starts a new verse, thirty one pages of it."

"It must have taken ages," said Pip, horrified at the thought, but he was beginning to get a bit fed-up with the book. He went over to where Timothy and Gramps were busy collecting the rest of Peter's things, and stowing them in the cupboards in his van. He started helping them and Gramps asked him to tell them again the story of the evening in the museum, when Beth had hidden from the intruder. Gramps had heard it during their interview with the police, but Timothy hadn't. They hadn't liked to mention it earlier, because they didn't want to worry their grandparents. Timothy was really surprised that they had suspected Grey Wolf.

"He would never do anything to harm you," he said. "He has been watching out for you all the time you have been here. He was telling me last night that when you first arrived he sensed that you may be in danger."

"He was certainly right about that," said Gramps. "If he hadn't been there last night, I don't know what might have happened." He shook his head, and ruffled his fingers through Pip's hair, much to his grandson's annoyance.

Nanna and Beth continued to look through the exercise book.

"The handwriting practice certainly took up a lot of pages," said Nanna, coming to the centre of the book, where at last the writing stopped. She was just about to pass it to the guys to pack into the van, when she flicked to the back of the book.

"Oh, my!" she exclaimed, in surprise, "Now this is quite different."

She showed Beth; and the guys, who had heard her, and were soon standing around, too.

"This looks like a journal," said Nanna, quickly glancing at a page or two.

"What?" asked Beth. "You mean it's another diary?" she said, thinking of the diary they had found last year.

"No, no!" Nanna said, immediately, shaking her head. "It's nothing like the other one you found. Elizabeth had taken great care writing her diary; this one is more like someone writing a few thoughts down on paper."

When they looked, they saw that the back page had the name Betsy Davis written at the top, and it was followed by quite a few more pages, written in the same childlike letters as those at the front of the book. Although the letters were easy to read Nanna realised that the old-fashioned style of the wording would make it difficult to read aloud. She was also conscious of the fact that the Rendezvous field was almost empty, now. Everything was ready for them to leave the site and return to the house.

"How about," she suggested to Beth, "If you take this into your bedroom tonight, and then tomorrow morning you can have a good read of what it says and you can tell us all about it." She knew that Beth was eager to have a go at solving this part of the mystery. She still enjoyed reading far more than Pip did.

Everyone thought that seemed to be the best idea, especially as they were all getting hungry and they were planning to go out to the pizza restaurant once they had unloaded the vehicles, back at the house.

At the restaurant they were discussing their findings, and Nanna mentioned the handwriting practice in the book they had found.

This gave Zac all the inspiration he needed for the bedtime story that night.

They settled on the porch, in the same seats they had used on their very first day, which now seemed ages ago. In reality it was less than two weeks since they left England.

Zac began. "The long, hot and horrible day was drawing to an end. They were glad of the cool of the evening after the heat of the day. But they both knew that as well as the gentle, cool breeze coming into the garden, someone else would be coming, too. Someone who came every evening, but tonight they didn't want to see him and they certainly didn't want him to see them. They looked under the deepening shadows of the trees for the darkest place to hide, and waited in fear.

"At last they heard the sound of footsteps approaching, and a voice calling, 'Where are you?' They kept very still and did not answer, but somehow they knew that it would only be moments before they were found."[7]

Beth was reminded of the time she had hidden in the ballroom, but they all enjoyed Zac's version of this, the story of Adam and Eve in the Garden of Eden.

"They chose to disobey God," said Bella May, "And were afraid of the consequences."

"I would have been too," said Timothy. "There are always consequences to be dealt with, when we have done wrong. Just look at Peter, locked up in jail. I can't believe how much we were taken in by him."

"It's always sad when people you trust let you down," said Nanna.

"I suppose that's how God felt about Adam and Eve," added Gramps. "After all, they were his friends, too, and they had disappointed him."

On that rather sad note, they all went to bed.

14

The Runaway

When Beth woke early the next morning her first thought was of Peter's exercise book and its contents. Then as she reached over to get it from the bedside table her eyes were drawn to the gold edging on the pages of her Bible, which seemed to be gleaming in the morning sun. She and Pip had been reading a little from their new Bibles most mornings, often racing each other to find the place of the bedtime story. She smiled over at Pip's sleeping form, and thought she would beat him that morning.

The story was easy to find, as it was nearly at the beginning of the Bible. She found herself reading a little further into chapter 4, the story of the murder of Abel, by his jealous brother Cain.

After breakfast Beth had spent most of the morning in the library hunched over the journal. As well as reading through the handwritten pages at the back she had made another little discovery. Tucked in between the last two pages were a couple of other newspaper cuttings. She made notes about her findings, to tell the others.

At last she was ready to share her conclusions with the rest of them. Timothy had taken the jewels out of the safe and she arranged the jewels in front of her, together with the writing case and the newspaper cuttings. Everyone was eager to hear what she had found in the old school book but they were surprised when a rather sad faced Beth announced that she thought she had solved the mystery.

They all gathered around. She explained that the entries in the journal were quite brief, so although it hadn't taken her long to read them through, she thought that it might be better to tell the story in her own words.

"It will probably be a bit more interesting than if I just read out what Betsy wrote," she said, thinking of how much they had all enjoyed the bedtime stories, recently. The storytellers had taken the facts from the Bible and then really made the characters come alive. She thought she would like to do that with the people from the notebook.

Beth told them that the journal belonged to a lady called Betsy Davis. She and her family had lived in the little village of Howarth, in the Yorkshire Dales in the nineteenth century. Beth stopped and pointed to the pages in the journal. "It's all in here," she said, "On the pages at the back of the handwriting practice.

"Betsy was one of three children," Beth continued her story. "She had an older brother called Harold and a younger sister, Rosemary. Betsy was always jealous of her younger sister, who had pretty blonde hair, and bright blue eyes. Everyone seemed to like Rosemary the best, and she was also their mother's favourite.

"Betsy and their brother had to work in the local mill, which was where their father worked, too. It was very hard work. Their mother didn't want 'her little Rosemary' to go there, so somehow she managed to get her a job as a maid at the Hall, the big house just outside the village. Betsy became even more jealous of her.

"Rosemary was determined to make the best of this new job. She had started by working in the kitchens," Beth told them. "She only got one day off a month, and would come home, eagerly telling her family all about her new place. She worked hard and soon became one of the under housemaids, and then something I'm not sure about," said Beth, looking over at Nanna.

She pointed out a word.

"Ah!" said Nanna; "I'm not surprised you didn't know that one. It says she became the 'tweeny', that is the maid who worked part-time downstairs and part-time in the upper floors, as chambermaid."

"Do you know," said Bella May, who was interested in life in old English houses. "I always wondered about that word. I have come across it in my reading, so a 'tweeny' was someone who worked between the floors of the house. It's a good descriptive word."

"Well, do go on, Beth," encouraged Zac, "You're turning into a good storyteller. Do carry on."

Beth blushed; that was high praise, coming from Zac, who was such a good storyteller himself. "Well," she continued, "Rosemary hoped one day to become upper housemaid, or even the lady's maid."

"A very important job," nodded Nanna.

"In February 1862," Beth checked the date in the journal, "It appears that Rosemary was sent home in trouble. She had done something so bad that she would never be allowed to go back to the Hall again. It doesn't say in here what she had done, because I don't think she told her family what it was. It says that she had been given 'no references'. What does that mean?" Beth asked.

"When you leave a job," said Gramps, "Your employer usually gives you a 'reference', a paper for you to give to your next job, telling them how good your work has been. Without a reference there was no possibility of Rosemary getting another job as a maid with another local family."

"Right," said Beth. "Rosemary didn't give them an explanation for this; she simply told her family that the other maids were jealous of her, and had told lies about her to her employers."

"I bet her mum wasn't very pleased," said Pip.

"Well," continued Beth, "That's what I would have thought, and although Betsy says that she didn't believe her sister, she says their mother took Rosemary at her word, and welcomed her back into the family home. As she had brought a little money that she had been saving each month from her wages, her mother even said that she didn't immediately need to start looking for another job, much to Betsy's annoyance."

"I bet she was furious!" said Pip.

"Let's get on with the story," said Gramps, smiling over at Pip.

Beth continued, "Rosemary had not been home long when one day Betsy woke up very early in the morning. The sisters were sharing the room they'd shared as children, but Betsy soon realised that Rosemary was not in bed. Betsy pulled a blanket over her nightdress and went out to the back of the house, where the outside toilet was. They called it a midden," said Beth, looking over at Nanna.

"Yes, that's right," she said.

"As she walked down the path towards the midden," Beth went on, "Betsy heard Rosemary being sick. Quickly Betsy ran back to the bedroom and pretended to be asleep when her sister came back indoors.

"Lying there in the darkness, listening to Rosemary's sleeping breaths, Betsy gloated over the fact that she suspected that her 'perfect sister' was going to have a baby. She decided to wait a few days to see if this was true. Meanwhile she was determined to spy on her sister at every opportunity.

"A day or two later both girls went to Bradford market together on Betsy's half day. It was not long before Rosemary gave Betsy the slip, going off on her own. Betsy had been half expecting this, so she had played along, letting her sister apparently lose her easily, but in fact she was watching exactly where she went, and secretly following.

"Rosemary had walked through some of the alleyways by the side of the market, and finally climbed up the short staircase outside a small shop."

Beth stopped for a moment, and pointed to a word on the page.

Nanna looked. "A pawnbrokers shop," she said.

"I wasn't sure what that was," said Beth.

"Ah!" said Gramps, "That's a bit complicated. It's a place where you can take something that is very valuable, and pawn it. That means the owner of the shop will give you some money, not nearly as much as it is really worth. Then he will keep the valuables, until you can afford to buy them back from him, but you would then have to pay a lot more than he originally gave you. That's how he makes his money. Then if you don't collect the valuables, 'redeem' them, it is called, after a certain amount of time, they belong to the shop and he can sell them for a lot of money."

"I wonder what the valuable things were that Rosemary was taking," asked Pip.

"I wonder," said Nanna, with a twinkle in her eyes.

Beth took up the story. "Betsy watched from the shadows, and then slipped back to the market, as though unaware of her sister's disappearance."

"She's really sneaky, isn't she?" asked Pip.

"Jealousy can make you do all sorts of horrible things," said Zac. "Remember the story of Joseph, we had the other day?"

The children nodded. Beth thought of the story she had read that morning, too.

"A week or so later," she continued, "Betsy again woke up to find the bedroom empty. This time she spoke to Rosemary, as she tried to creep back into bed, asking if it was true that she was having a baby. Rosemary wouldn't speak to her, which made Betsy so mad that she blurted out her suspicions as the family were having breakfast."

"She's a bit of a tell-tale, isn't she?" said Pip.

"Yes, indeed," added Zac.

"You're right about that," continued Beth. "Anyway, their father stormed out of the house on his way to the early shift in the mill, telling Rosemary that he wanted her out of the house before he came home that evening. Betsy used a strange expression," said Beth, again pointing to the words. "He said she was never to 'darken their doors again'. What does that mean?" she asked.

"Never come home, I expect," offered Pip.

"That's it," agreed Gramps. "You see, your shadow falls on the door, darkening it, when you come knocking, if the sun is in the right direction. That's where the expression comes from."

"What did her mother say?" asked Nanna.

"She collapsed," Beth went on. "She was shattered. Betsy even mentioned that her hair went white overnight, and she was never the same again. Betsy had to go to work that day but she only had a short shift to do, so at lunchtime she returned to the house. Her mother was crying by the fire and told her that Rosemary was upstairs, packing. Betsy quietly climbed up the steps to make sure her sister didn't take any of her things. As she was going upstairs she heard some banging coming from their room. She crept further up, determined to continue spying on her, and saw Rosemary bending over the table, with a hammer and a chisel in her hands.

"As soon as she saw Betsy, Rosemary furtively pulled an old shawl over the table, hiding what she had been doing. She hovered about on the landing, hoping to see something more, but she didn't.

"Rosemary soon had her small bundle of belongings packed and went back down to the kitchen. Her mother reached up to the old tin where she kept the family savings, and handed her a few coins, but Rosemary threw them back in her mother's face, saying, 'I don't need your pathetic savings! We'll manage without your help. We will have a new life and a new start, in a new world, you see if we don't!' Then she slammed out of the house, and was never to be seen again," Beth said, dramatically.

Everyone sat in stunned silence, taking in the facts of the story.

"The writing finishes soon after that," concluded Beth, "Although sometime later Betsy records the fact that she discovered two links of gold chain, under the rug by the bedroom table, and a few months after that puts the date of her own wedding to the local schoolmaster, Edward Barrowclough."

Beth paused, expectantly, and was gratified to hear Zac gasp.

15

The Thief

"Edward Barrowclough?" Zac repeated, "Do you think . . . surely that is quite an unusual name, isn't it? Barrowclough?" he said again. "Do you think that she could be related . . . related to Peter?" he asked.

Beth nodded. "That's what I thought! And there is something else," she added, sadly. "Tucked inside the journal were these."

She took out two more old newspaper cuttings. One had a short article and a black and white drawing of an ornate necklace. The headline read 'Regency Rubies Stolen from Howarth Hall'.

"Stolen!" said Pip, horrified.

"Well I never!" exclaimed Gramps. "Regency Rubies, no wonder they look so special."

"But," interrupted Pip, "Does that mean that the rubies we found had been stolen?"

"It looks that way," said Beth.

"But if they are the same jewels, how did the rubies from Yorkshire end up in our blanket box in Astoria?" questioned Timothy.

They all looked bemused. "I . . . I don't really know," Beth hesitated.

"Oh, no!" sighed Zac, realising what she meant. "No, not our Rose!"

Everyone except Beth looked blankly at him.

"We knew she came from England," said Timothy, "And we didn't know much more about her than that."

"I know," continued Zac, sadly shaking his head, "But if this Rosemary is our Rose it means . . ."

Pip interrupted him. "Oh, no!" he said, suddenly understanding why Zac was so sad. "It means she stole the rubies!"

"I'm afraid it looks like that," said Zac.

"I almost wish that we hadn't found all this," said Bella May, voicing what they were all feeling. "What a shame that our wonderful Rose turns out to be nothing more than a thieving little maid, who ran away from her family to build her life on the proceeds of a precious heirloom stolen from her employers."

"No wonder you looked so sad," said Zac, looking over to Beth, "When you started to tell us your story. I think you had begun to guess the truth, hadn't you?"

"I'm afraid I couldn't think of another explanation," she admitted.

A sad silence settled around the library table for a moment or two.

They looked down at the picture.

"There seems to be a lot more gold in the drawing than we found in the bag," said Pip.

"Well, we know she used some for her ticket," said Beth.

"She must have used more for the journey west," said Bella May.

"And in setting up the timber yards," added Timothy.

"That's right," put in Nanna. "A maid who had no job would need something to use for money."

"What does the other newspaper cutting say?" Pip eventually asked, referring to the other, smaller piece of newsprint in Beth's hand. She passed it over to their grandmother.

'Double Trouble at Howarth Hall' read Nanna. "It tells how a few months after the theft of the heirloom necklace, belonging to the old Lady Howarth, there is another tragedy for the family when young Lord John is killed in a coaching accident whilst journeying on the road west of Bradford. It's almost the same as the one we read yesterday."

"But this one was with Peter's things," said Pip, "So he must have known about the accident and the jewels. He must have been tracking the necklace all the way from England."

Gramps added, "That first day in the museum, he told us he had been following the trail of those early explorers, Lewis and Clark. That must have just been a cover story. All the time he must have been trying to find the rubies."

"Yes, I suppose so," said Zac.

"Wait a minute," said Pip, "Didn't you say you had a break-in just before he started working for you?"

"We sure did!" answered Zac. "I wonder if he was responsible for that, too?"

"And then," added Pip, "Since he obviously didn't find them in the break-in, he must have decided to work here, so that he would have a better chance to search."

"You've got something, there," said Zac, remembering. "Now I come to think of it, often when I would come in when he had been here on his own, I would find things had been moved around; not big things, just little things. I assumed it had been the cleaner, but now I come to think about it, it only began after Peter joined us."

"But he seemed so nice," said Bella May. "He was so friendly, even that first time we met him. Do you remember Tim, how concerned he was about your Dad needing some extra help, after the burglary? Oh, my goodness," she added, "Even then he was scheming!"

"And just pretending to be friendly," added Gramps, disappointedly.

"What a thoroughly nasty piece of work," said Timothy.

"So now we know," said Nanna, picking up the journal, "That Peter has used the information in here to follow the trail of Rosemary, from West Yorkshire right over to the west coast of America."

"And she came from near Howarth Hall, eh?" asked Gramps. "That's just a few miles outside Bradford, isn't it?"

"It is that," replied Nanna.

"You mean, you guys know the very places that Betsy talks about?" asked Zac.

"We used to live fairly near there, years ago," Gramps replied. "In fact, that was the area Peter and I were discussing. He came from there, too. I didn't think anything of it at the time."

"No, you wouldn't," said Zac, "We were all taken in by him, I'm afraid. But that means that you know some of the places in Betsy's journal, does it?"

"Well, we've certainly been to Bradford market," said Gramps, "But I've never noticed pawnbrokers there."

"There used to be a big mill out Howarth way," added Nanna. "Lots of the locals would have worked there."

"But not 'our Rosemary', of course," added Beth, quoting from the journal.

"No," said Nanna. "She was a maid in the big house until she had to leave."

"Because she stole the rubies," said Beth.

"Well, I don't know about that," interrupted Gramps. "I've been thinking. The family would never let her get away with the jewels. If her employers knew that she had stolen the rubies, wouldn't they have had her arrested?"

"Of course they would!" said Zac, looking happier than he had for a while.

"But she was sent home in trouble," insisted Beth. "If she didn't steal the rubies, why did she have to go home?"

"Oh, my!" said Nanna, suddenly, "She was sent home for the most common reason pretty maids were sent away from wealthy young men in those days." She looked around the table.

Bella May was the first to realise what Nanna meant. "Because she was having a baby!" she exclaimed.

"That's right. She was expecting a baby," said Nanna, who had been re-examining the ticket that had been in the writing case. She calculated the months. "A baby who would probably have been born after her voyage on board this liner. She was sent home early in the year," Nanna went on, "And the ticket was for April; the journey would have taken quite a while."

"Yes indeed!" said Zac, "Depending on the weather, it could take a good few weeks, in those days."

""That must be the journey to the New World, that Betsy mentions Rosemary talking about," said Beth. "She said 'we' were going to have a new start," said Beth. "She must have meant her and the baby."

"Well now," said Gramps, "That might just explain things. If she wasn't married, but was going to have a baby, that could well be the reason she changed her name."

"Ready for her new life," added Beth.

"But just a minute," said Timothy, "I know that we are all wanting to find a reason why Rose can't be the thief, but, let's face it, we have the rubies here. If she didn't steal them, how on earth did she get them?"

Once again a stunned silence settled around the table. At last Zac shook his head. "Well, we can't sit around chatting forever," he said. "We wanted to know more about Rose, and you have certainly found out a lot more than we knew before." Pip and Beth nodded, but they weren't feeling happy about their findings at the moment.

Later that day Zac had to go back to the museum to return some of the articles that they had used on the Rendezvous. He asked the children if they would like to go with him, and they were happy to.

The lawn looked quite empty as they walked up, now that all the Rendezvous things had been taken down. They went into the entrance hall. On the table were copies of the local newspapers, reporting all the exciting events of the past week. Pip and Beth helped Zac to return things, and then Pip felt that he wanted a bit of time on his own.

He went out into the sunshine, across the grass to the edge of the river. He picked up a pebble and skimmed it over the water. He began to think again about Rosemary Davis, or Rose Davidson, and what they had found out about her. She seemed to have stolen those amazing rubies that they had found. How could she steal those jewels, if she was a follower of Jesus? It was all a rather disappointing end to the Mystery of the Museum. He scuffed his shoes among the stones, and wearily turned back to find Beth.

She wasn't in the hall, so he wandered into the shop. She wasn't there so he began to search the lower rooms. After walking into the office where Isaac had learned about the business of the timber yard he noticed a door in the corner. He opened it, and to his surprise, entered the library, among the bookshelves, by the side door, from a different direction that they hadn't seen before.

Coming in this way, the first thing he noticed was the huge mirror, hanging over the fireplace. In it was the reflection of the two dummies of Rose and Isaac. The sunlight was streaming in through the window behind them, and although they seemed to be in shadow, Pip was struck by the intent way the model of Rose seemed to be looking at something. He couldn't quite see, so he moved around the corner of the shelf, still concentrating on the image in the mirror.

What he saw was his sister. She was standing by the fireplace, holding, of all things, a newspaper. He could only see the left side of her, and the front page of the paper she was reading in the mirror. Pip took a step closer and focused more on the reflection, and then suddenly called out:

"Hold still! Don't move!"

Beth almost jumped out of her skin. She hadn't heard him arrive, and wasn't aware that there was another entrance to the library.

"Where did you come from?" she asked, putting her arms down and folding the paper.

"That doesn't matter," said Pip, crossly. "I said don't move, and you've changed the reflection, now."

"The reflection?" she questioned, "What reflection?"

"There was something important in the reflection of the newspaper," he said. "Hold it up again!" he ordered.

Beth did as she was told. "Like this?" she asked, opening it again to the middle pages where she had been reading the account of the Rendezvous, and trying to find her family in the photographs, which wasn't hard, because both reporter and photographer had been very interested in the Treasure Hunters from England.

"Yes, keep it up!" Pip demanded. "Some of those letters are exactly the same as the ones on Rose's sampler."

The headline read: GREY WOLF MAKES IT RIGHT but the reflection looked almost identical to some of the strange lettering on the sampler, that they hadn't been able to understand. Pip looked again at the reflection, then back at the newspaper. It was only when he looked again into the mirror that he could see the similarity to the embroidered lettering.

By now Beth was intrigued, and her arms were beginning to ache, holding the paper up. "What do you mean?" she asked, "Let me see!"

"OK," Pip strode across to her. "You'll need to stand just where I was," he pointed at the corner of the shelves. Then he stood exactly where she had been and lifted the closed newspaper, so that only the front page was visible to Beth. "Don't look at me," he insisted, "Just look at the reflection!"

Beth did, and what she saw reminded her immediately of what she had copied into her drawing book.

"Oh, Pip!" she exclaimed, "I think you're onto something, there. Let's check it out!" Straight away she took the drawing pad out of the bag she was carrying over her shoulder. She took it to an empty table and she and Pip examined it. He placed the folded newspaper next to it, showing the headlines.

"The paper says that Grey Wolf 'MAKES IT RIGHT', doesn't it?" said Pip.

Beth looked at the entry in her book.

T H ? I ? T I ? ? A M

"But if the strange letters on the sampler are reflections," Beth answered, "They are very similar. We need to start reading at the end of the line. Those three words are just the same, except that there is no 's', is there?"

"So it must just say 'MAKE IT RIGHT', mustn't it?" said Pip. "So if Rose made this embroidery as a clue for Isaac, she must have meant for him to make something right." Pip looked straight at Beth.

"That could surely mean," she said, excitedly, "That she wanted him to put right something that she had done wrong."

"Something like stealing the rubies!" he said.

"Just like Zacchaeus!" she replied.

"Zacchaeus?" asked Pip.

"Yes, you know!" said Beth, "He gave back all the things that he had stolen!"

"In her favourite story, of course!" said Pip. "We must go and tell Zac, he will be pleased that she wanted to do the right thing in the end."

"He will," said Beth.

They rushed into the hallway, calling out for Zac, carrying the newspaper, the copy of the words from the sampler, and almost tripping over each other in their eagerness. As soon as Zac realised what they were talking about, and this time they were so excited that they were talking on top of each other, both trying to explain together, he went upstairs to the bedroom and brought the sampler down. They took everything into the coffee shop, and were soon eating one of their favourite ice creams, going over all the facts again.

"So what you are saying," said Zac, "Is that at the very end of her life Rose wants to return the rubies, but she knows that she is going to die soon."

"That's right!" said Pip. "She probably even realised that she would die before Isaac came home again."

"So she decides to leave Isaac some clues to their whereabouts, in the embroidery she is doing," added Beth, between licks of the ice-cream.

"I always thought it was a strange gift for a boy," Pip said.

"But it was full of clues, riddles," said Beth. "Just like the riddles they used to solve together."

"Let's have another look at that," said Zac, placing the sampler between them on the metal table in the sun.

"At the top is the poem," he began, "Which talks about the figures on the clock. And we said the last line, 'Tempus fugit,' which is Latin for 'time flies' could have two meanings. Rose would have known that Isaac was learning Latin at school, so it could help him to find the key in the clock, and could also remind him that she knew that her time on this earth was flying fast."

Pip nodded. "And at the moment we are thinking about the fact that she made this at the very end of her life."

"That's right." said Beth.

"Underneath the poem is the picture of the key," said Pip, "And we found the key in the little drawer at the bottom of the clock." Pip looked again at the embroidery, and then over to Zac. "Now then, I remember you saying that Rose hated the herb rosemary, and yet all around the picture of the house she has sewn leaves and flowers from that very plant. We said that could be important, and it is."

"That should have led Isaac to look for someone called Rosemary," said Beth, "And we know now that she used to be called Rosemary Davis."

"So that's the top of the picture." Pip went on, "Down the right-hand side of the house are the numbers 10 to 1, going downwards."

"And we worked out that the number 1 could also be read as I in Isaac," said Beth, pointing at it.

"Then comes the Bible reference to the Zacchaeus story," put in Pip.

"But the particular verse," added Beth, "That Rose mentions is verse 8, the one that talks about Zacchaeus returning the money he had stolen."

"I'm with you," said Zac, following what they were saying. "It's funny how we all just thought of the whole story as being important to her, when she had actually picked out that particular verse."

"That's right, and it just leaves the last three letters on that column," said Beth, reading them, "4 M E."

"For me!" exclaimed Pip, suddenly remembering the chalk letters on the blackboard in the schoolroom. "You know! Like the puzzle on the blackboard!"

"Of course," said Beth, "Why didn't we see that before?" she mused.

"Sometimes just looking at things again makes us see them in a new way," explained Zac.

"Exactly!" said Pip, "And that's just what happened in the library." He folded the newspaper that Beth had been reading, and placed it on the table, next to the sampler. Now that he had shown them how he had recognised the stitched lettering as reflections of real letters they could see that Rose's embroidery really finished with a reflection of the words MAKE IT RIGHT.

"So Rose is giving Isaac the clues to make it right for her," Pip said.

"But unfortunately," said Zac, "He didn't."

"How do you mean?" asked Beth.

"Well, "answered Zac, "From all we have been able to see, Isaac never understood Rose's clues, and so he was never able to make it right for her."

"That's it!" said Pip. "He couldn't make it right, because he never deciphered the clues. We've solved them now, so perhaps we should make it right for her," he added, smiling.

"Make it right for Rose?" asked Beth, not really understanding what Pip was meaning.

"Ye-e-es," said Pip slowly, enjoying the fact that he had worked something out before his sister. "She wanted him to give the rubies back. He didn't. Perhaps we should."

"Give them back?" she asked, still bewildered, "Who would we give them back to?" she repeated.

"You mean," said Zac, following Pip's logic, "We should give the jewels back to the descendants of Lord and Lady Howarth, in England?"

"Ye-e-es," Pip said again.

"Oh, I see!" said Beth, at last. "She wanted him to return them, so we should return them instead." She thought for a moment, then asked, "But how on earth could we do that?"

"How indeed?" asked Zac, getting up. "We shall have to see," he said, "But for now, I think the rest of them will be wondering where on earth we have got to. Time for home, I think."

The children picked up all the things they needed, and they all went off to share their discoveries.

That evening as they were sitting on the porch Bella May said she had just the story to finish the day for them. Timothy had already decided that tomorrow morning he would set up an Internet search for the family of Lord and Lady Howarth.

"Well, today," Bella May began, "We are waiting to contact some people who our family has not been in contact with for many, many years. That reminded me of a story in the Bible.

"During the night," she began, "Jacob got up secretly and took his family across the river to safety. Then he went back for his possessions, but while he was alone in the camp he became aware that someone was watching him. He glanced over his shoulder, and sure enough he could just make out a lighter shape among the darker shadows. It looked like a man, and yet somehow it seemed to gleam with light from inside itself. Who could it be?"

Pip and Beth couldn't help remembering how they had felt that Grey Wolf was watching them. They had been right about that, but wrong about his reasons. They settled back to listen to a story that they had never heard before. They were certainly captivated as Bella May told how Jacob wrestled with the angel, on the night before he met up again with his long-lost brother.[8]

16

Truth Revealed

There was a real air of excitement about the place, as Bella May suggested that rather than clearing the breakfast things, they all go into Timothy's office, to see what they could find on an Internet search for Howarth Hall. They didn't have long to wait. When the search was completed, up popped a photograph of a huge grey stone building, three storeys high, with a sweeping drive going up to it. Pip was the first to voice what they were all thinking.

"That looks almost exactly like the house on Rose's sampler. They must surely be the same place!" he said.

Beth ran to get the embroidery, and by the time she returned, Timothy had already decided to try to make contact with the family. There was a web site address at the bottom of the page.

"Now don't hold your breath!" he said. "These things can sometimes take ages to get a reply. Often people don't update them for weeks at a time. We may not even hear anything until you are back in England."

The children looked disappointed.

"We'll let you know," added Timothy, "As soon as we hear."

They settled down to enjoy their last few days, and were really surprised when only the next day Timothy answered the phone, and came onto the porch where they were all enjoying some of Bella May's homemade lemonade and chunks of crispy red apple.

"Well, that was a surprise," he said. "That was a call from a Mr Jones, solicitors from Bradford, England. Apparently they have offices in Portland, Oregon, and are sending their representative out to visit us, this afternoon!"

As you can imagine, everyone was there, watching as a large black car drew up to the gates! Two men in smart black suits got out and came up the drive; the older man was carrying a beautifully made leather briefcase.

They all went into the lounge, where Bella May had already set the coffee percolator going and in no time at all drinks had been passed around and they settled back to listen, as Mr. Jones Senior began.

"Five years ago," he told them, "The last Earl of Howarth died, aged 82. He had no known living relatives. My brother, William Jones, still runs our head office in Bradford. Our firm have been solicitors to the Howarths for many years. As the executors of his will, we were charged with trying to trace anyone with a claim to the title and inheritance. Going through the family papers we came across this letter, which was lodged with our firm. It is dated 1862." He handed the letter over for Zac who read it out for them all to hear.

> *Dearest Papa and Mama*
> *By the time you read this I shall be on my way across the Atlantic, to join my darling Rosemary in our new life together.*
> *I realise that you do not approve of my intention to marry her, but that will not stop me!*
> *If it had been just the two of us, I would have left you without taking a penny of my inheritance; however she is carrying our beloved child, so I told her to take the Regency Rubies. Grandmamma Hardman bequeathed them to me for my wedding. I am sure she would have approved of my beautiful Rosemary, as she herself was only a governess, when Grandpapa fell in love with her.*
> *I do not expect that we shall ever meet again!*
> *Respectfully Your Son*
> *John Howarth Esq*

The children looked across at Zac in amazement.

"So John intended to come to the States and be with Rose!" Beth said.

"It would seem so!" said Mr Jones. "At first we couldn't find much out about Rosemary. Later we looked through the employment registers. One Rosemary Davis worked in the house from 1858 to 1862, rising quickly from scullery maid, through to housemaid, and assistant lady's maid. She left in February 1862 'for family reasons' apparently!"

"When we received your e mail, things began to fit together," young Mr. Jones added, "But we are still not sure how you managed to find a connection between your Rose Davidson, and the mysterious Rosemary, from the letter."

Zac smiled, "Well, we didn't really find anything," he said, looking over at Pip and Beth. "It's all down to these two young detectives from England."

The children beamed.

"Perhaps Mr. Jones and his son might like to see the evidence," suggested Bella May, knowing full well that the children had spent most of the morning getting everything together. They went into the kitchen and brought back a large tray. Pip had even covered it with a bright red and white cloth. He laid the tray on the coffee table.

"Da, dah!" he said, removing the cloth with a flourish.

Everyone smiled, but the solicitors both moved their chairs forward, eager to get a better view.

On the tray were the various items that had led to the solving of the mystery, and the gentlemen were amazed as the children picked up the items in order, explaining how they had solved the mystery.

There was the embroidered sampler, with Rose's Bible open at the story of Zacchaeus. The children had even taken some photographs of things that were too big to carry, like the clock. They had a picture of the lettering, which matched that of the sampler, and another picture with the secret drawer open, which they had put beside the silver key, with the tag saying 'my chest'. Then there was another photo, this time of the sea chest, but the interior, with its secret compartment, was difficult to see, so Pip explained about the carving of the letter Z, before showing the writing case. The Joneses were very interested in the contents of the case, and showed everyone how similar the crest that

Rose had drawn was to the official crest on John's letter. They looked long and hard at the ticket for the liner, and Mr. Jones Senior pointed to the word Liverpool.

"Liverpool," he said, "The port closest to Bradford, for a journey to the New World."

His son was thinking through some of the new facts that they had about Rosemary. He picked up the newspaper reporting John's death. "She must have read this," he said, sadly shaking her head. "She must have been heart-broken and decided that, although he couldn't go with her to the new life he had planned for them, she would still make the journey and build a life for herself and for John's baby."

"But where would a young woman," asked Mr. Jones Senior, knowing the answer already, "Who was only a lowly servant at the Hall, get the money from to do that?"

"I think this might be the answer to that," said Beth, holding out the blue velvet bag.

Although the solicitors had been expecting to see the broken ruby necklace, because Timothy had mentioned it in the e mails, they gasped, as Beth tipped the jewels onto a black satin scarf, which Bella May had carefully placed in front of the sunniest window. The gems sparkled and shone, showing a deep red glow, as the sunbeams lit up the depths of colour inside them. The black scarf behind them only made them seem brighter than ever.

"The Regencies!" exclaimed Mr. Jones.

"They are awesome," said his son, leaning forward to get a closer look.

Mr. Jones Senior reached out and reverently took hold of the largest ruby that had been broken completely out of its chain.

"To think that at last I get a chance to hold this in my hand!" he said.

Young Mr. Jones picked up some of the shattered pieces of gold, and let them trickle though his fingers. "A pawnbroker would be happy to give money on this, enough for a new beginning," he said. "Plenty for her to provide travel money and still enough to start her business here at the timber yard."

Zac sighed. "I expect you will be taking them away with you today," he said, rather sadly, "But I wondered if we could get a few photos, before you do?"

"Taking them away?" repeated Mr. Jones, puzzled. "But why should we be taking them away?"

"But, Father," his son interrupted, "We haven't explained yet about the heir."

"Oh, my goodness," exclaimed the older gentleman, "We were so fascinated by your story, we haven't told you ours. Please forgive us."

He carefully replaced the ruby with the others and settled back in his chair. "We came this afternoon because we have been charged by the terms of Lord Howarth's will to locate the heir, the heir of the estate, the heir to the title, and of course, the legal owner of all the heirlooms of the family, including these magnificent jewels." He smiled directly at Zac. "And from what your son mentioned on the e mail to my son, I believe I am looking at him!"

"I beg your pardon," said Zac, taken aback, "What . . . whatever do you mean?"

Young Mr. Jones took up the story. "As my Father said, Lord Howarth died without leaving any living family. So in his will he insisted that our firm be responsible for tracing anyone from his family line. He wanted the estate go to them, rather than being handed over to the government."

"It seems more than likely," continued Mr. Jones Senior, "That you are in fact the descendant of Rosemary Davis and John Howarth. If that can be proved to my satisfaction, then I shall inform my brother in England that I have found the lost heir of the Earl of Howarth."

Zac could hardly take it in.

"That was why," his son continued, "We were so interested in your account," he looked over at Pip and Beth, "Of how you solved the mystery, not so much on account of where the rubies were hidden, but of the fact that Rose Davidson was in reality Rosemary Davis, of Yorkshire, England."

"Wow!" said Pip.

"So that discovery was even more important than the rubies?" asked Beth, in amazement.

Mr. Jones Senior nodded vigorously, "Oh, yes," he said. "You see Rosemary was actually given those rubies by the legal owner of them. It seems that she may not have realised that, which is why she obviously felt so guilty about taking the necklace, and why she wanted her son to make it right."

Zac smiled at last. "Well, I for one am really glad about that. I can't really get my head around anything else, just yet, but I am glad my great-grandfather's beloved mother was not just a nasty little thief."

At that moment, Timothy walked back into the room, carrying the family Bible from the museum. No one had noticed him leave.

"I had a feeling that this might help," he said.

He sat down on the sofa, between the solicitors, and opened the Bible to the front pages, where it listed the members of his family, with the dates of their births, deaths and marriages.

"Exactly!" said Mr. Jones Senior.

The conversations ran on about the various members of the Davidson family. It was now obvious to everyone that the reason Rose had never written a surname for the top two names, John and Rose, was because she changed her name, and didn't want to show that Isaac was illegitimate.

"That's why I could never find any information about John Davidson," smiled Timothy. "There never was anyone called that!"

"But now that we, or rather you," said Mr. Jones Senior, looking over at the children, "Have cleared up the mystery of the first two names, John and Rose, all these other details in here can easily be checked in the records office, and I am sure that that will prove that you, Zac, are indeed the long lost heir of the Howarth Estate, and legal owner of these beautiful rubies."

When Zac was sitting on the porch later that day, the truth about his inheritance was only just sinking in.

"Do you know," he said, "It reminds me of the man in the Bible with the unpronounceable name. He was a man who expected nothing good would come from meeting the king, but things turned out better than he could have anticipated. He had hoped to live out his days in hiding, but then one day he got the summons to go before the new king."[9]

Finale

The local Astoria paper ran the story the following day. The headlines read 'Heir to English fortune found at Centenary Celebrations', and in an interview with the children the reporter said, "These two are getting quite a reputation for solving mysteries!"

Finally as they all gathered together on the porch as usual, on their very last night in America, Zac had Rose's Bible open on his knee, as he sat once again between the children on the swing.

"We had the story of Zacchaeus, quite early on in our time together, but today I thought we would just start there, and think about a couple of people who have been part of the mystery you have been solving."

Zac had just finished speaking, when some newcomers arrived on the porch, after walking silently round the side of the house. Pip smiled over at Beth. A few days ago they would have thought the silent approach was sinister, but now they knew that that was the way Grey Wolf and his cub always moved around the forests. It was surprising how quietly Dancing Spring could move, too. Chairs were moved around to make room for them all to join the party.

"I was just going to talk about you," said Zac, as Grey Wolf settled on the floor, his wolf cub curled around his feet. "I have been thinking how meeting with Jesus changed Zacchaeus' life forever. It made him do things differently. He stopped doing the things that were wrong and gave away the money he had stolen.

"I thought that was very like the difference in Rose's life. She had taken the rubies, we know now that it was at John's suggestion that she took them, but she obviously felt guilty about it. When she became a Christian, just a few months before she died, she wanted to give back the things she felt she had stolen. Rose was asking Isaac to right the wrong she had done, just as Zac in the Bible put right the wrong he had done." Zac paused. "I guess Isaac just didn't see the clues."

The children nodded, then Beth cleared her throat. "Umm," she hesitated, looking over at Grey Wolf. "Sometimes when you get something wrong, you have to say sorry, don't you?"

Nanna immediately guessed what Beth meant. "That's a good thing to do," she said.

"Well," said Beth, glancing over at her brother, "I think Pip and I made a mistake about you, Grey Wolf," she said quietly, adding, "And I am very sorry."

"Me too!" said Pip, straight away. "We were completely wrong in thinking that you were an enemy. We are so sorry."

They received one of Grey Wolf's very rare smiles, which seemed to start at the corners of his mouth and then fill his whole face with a warm glow. "Thank you," he said. "Saying sorry is no easy thing to do. Thank you."

Pip looked over from the Indian to the cowboy. "But Zac," he asked, "Didn't you say there were two people connected to the mystery whose lives had been changed? You mentioned the difference in Rose . . ."

"I did," admitted Zac, looking over at his native friend.

"Hmm," nodded the Indian. "I think I know what Zac was going to tell you." He nodded again at Zac, and then looked straight at the children. "Getting to know Jesus really does change your life," he began, in his deep, almost musical voice.

It was the longest anyone there had heard him speak, and over the next few minutes he explained how growing up on the reservation he had not believed in God, but in the spirits of his ancestors. He told how a missionary had come one day, telling them the story of Jesus, and he had suddenly realised that he wanted to follow Jesus himself. He told them how there were things in his life that had not been right, and how he needed to make some changes, just like Zacchaeus and Rose. He gently smiled as he brought his story to a close.

"When we put things right with God," he concluded, "Then he can use us in amazing ways. When you two first arrived I felt God asking me to watch over you. Gradually I began to notice that I wasn't the only one keeping an eye on what you were doing, so when Peter had sprung his trap I was near enough to stop him."

"And very glad we were, too!" said Gramps, as everyone nodded in agreement.

"Well," said Pip, "We certainly are going to have some stories to tell, when we get home!"

THE END

The Bedtime Stories

Why not have a go at finding some of the bedtime stories for yourselves? Use a good modern translation of the Bible, something like the Good News Bible or the New Living Translation. In 'Mystery at the Manor' Nanna tells the children how to find a Bible reference for themselves. Let me remind you.

"It's like an address . . . it's easiest to start at the contents page to find where the reference begins . . . So for Matthew 2:1-12 find 'Matthew' in the list and turn to that page . . . 2 means Matthew chapter two; 1-12 means begin reading at verse one and continue until the end of verse twelve."

1	Chapter 1	Visitors in the Night	Matthew 2:1-12
2	Chapter 4	Through the leaves	Luke 19:1-14
3	Chapter 6	Jealousy	Genesis 37:3-36
4		The Builders	Matthew 7:24-27
5	Chapter 8	Singing at Midnight	Acts 16:16-40
6	Chapter 13	Throwing the Spear	1 Samuel 18:5-12
7		Hiding in the Garden	Genesis 3:1-24
8	Chapter 15	Stranger in the Night	Genesis 32:22-32
9	Chapter 16	The Crippled Prince	2 Samuel 9:1-13

Have you read the first Pip and Beth book
Mystery at the Manor?

In the grounds of an ancient Manor House a mystery has lain concealed for centuries. The accidental discovery of an old diary will lead Pip and Beth on a dangerous quest as they search for the hidden treasure and solve the Mystery at the Manor.

Lightning Source UK Ltd.
Milton Keynes UK
UKOW051011051211

183225UK00002B/2/P